MAGNIFICENT FAILURE

Patricia M. Robertson

Chapter 1

Times Square. New Year's Eve. Jake Alexander was one amid the swarming multitude waiting for the ball to drop. Another year had passed. So many balls had been dropped during his life. Sometimes they had dropped right into his lap, and he fumbled the play.

Lights glared at him and around him. Faces laughed on the big screens surrounding the square. All about him stood people with friends and family, people having fun, while he was alone. It hadn't always been that way. One time he had had a family too. One time he had had it all: home, wife, kids, and money—lots of it. But Jake had fumbled the play and lost the game.

Yet another New Year's Eve alone. Diane Price sat in front of the TV waiting for the Times Square ball to drop. Why didn't she just go to bed, she asked herself? But she knew why. She knew she wouldn't sleep. She'd lie awake waiting for her son to get home, worrying about him. Too many sleepless nights she had spent worrying about this boy-child soon to be a man, and worrying about his sister before him, and his dad before that, before he left them all.

So here she was, waiting for the ball to drop. It seemed she'd been waiting all her life. What was she waiting for? First, she had waited for her husband. Then she waited for and waited on her children. Now her life was half over, and it felt like it hadn't even begun. She had botched the first half. Will the next be any different, she wondered?

New Year's Eve in Times Square. Jake remembered when it had been different, all those years on Wall Street as an investment banker. He had completed his liberal arts degree to satisfy his interests, then went on to get an MBA from Kendall School of Business at Northwestern University to satisfy his need for income. He had married Laura while they were both undergrads. She had supported him while he went to Kendall, working full time so he could attend school full time. Then there were those crazy years as an associate, working long hours, establishing himself and climbing until he reached the coveted position of manager. Laura had been busy with their children and pursuing a degree as a tax accountant. Once their youngest started school full time, Laura was poised to land a good position in an accounting firm, as she too worked herself up the corporate ladder.

It had been fun at first, networking, making connections, manipulating numbers, making deals. Then there was 9/11. While no one close to him had died, people Jake had known, people he had worked with, were left behind in the rubble. He had listed their names on a piece of paper and left it on his desk as a reminder, his own tribute to those he had known.

He also remembered those individuals he had escorted out of the building when they were let go, the look of shock on their faces as they were notified, their offices cleaned out, and they were ushered out the door within an hour. Then as he rose up the ranks, he was the one making the decisions, leaving someone under him the messy task of giving them the bad news so he didn't have his sleep disturbed. This didn't work. Their faces came back to haunt him, disrupting his sleep.

He began to ask questions: What was he doing? Why? He found it harder and harder to look the other way when questionable deals came across his desk.

He didn't know exactly when it had happened. Seeds of discontent were sown that slowly took root and grew until he realized that not only could he not continue doing what he had been doing, he felt he needed to make restitution in some way.

He remembered that morning, the look his wife had given him.

"Why aren't you dressed for work?" Laura asked him while looking him up and down, reproach in her voice.

"I'm not going," Jake answered as he reached into the refrigerator for cream.

"Are you sick?"

"No, I'm just not going. I'm taking the day off. Let's play hooky, Laura, just you and me, like when we were kids. Remember?"

"Are you crazy, Jake?" Laura shook her head and walked to the kitchen sink to rinse coffee cups before placing them in the dishwasher.

"Wouldn't it be great to just blow off the day, like we used to? We could go to the beach, rent a dune buggy. Just for today. Wouldn't it be great?"

"If this is some sort of midlife crisis, Jake, then go out and buy yourself a Porsche, but don't drag me into this. I have way too much to do." Laura didn't even look at him in her haste to get past him and to the garage door. "If you aren't going to work, at least make yourself useful. Pick up the laundry at the dry cleaners, will you? I have to get the kids to school."

Jake watched his wife rush by, her hair pulled up at the nape of her neck into some kind of twist; she was elegant in her suit and high heels. He remembered a beautiful young girl, long blond hair blowing in the breeze off the lakeshore. She was still beautiful, but that seemed to be all she had in common with the young girl he remembered.

He sat at the kitchen counter in his jeans and a sweatshirt, coffee in hand, as his son and daughter walked around him. They fought over the last Pop-tart®, grabbed juice boxes for the road and their backpacks, and rushed out without a word to acknowledge Jake's existence.

"Guess I might as well go to work," he said to no one in particular.

"Don't forget the dry cleaning," his wife shouted back at him on her way out the door.

He went to work, told his secretary to cancel his morning appointments, closed the door to his office, and sat behind his desk. He picked up the list of names. The paper was well worn where he had fingered it over the years. That was when Jake knew he couldn't go on. He had already dropped out of Laura's life; he didn't know when, just knew it had happened, and all that was left was a shell.

He was a stranger to his children; the oldest was in college, the others soon to follow. All he had to do was make it final by leaving. It took him six months to take the leap, quit his job, and move out, but he did it. And now here he was.

How the mighty have fallen, the phrase resounded in his head. He wasn't sure where the saying had come from, but it seemed appropriate as he looked at where he was, how far he had fallen. And now here he was on another New Year's Eve, waiting for the ball to drop.

Diane had fallen asleep in the chair when she was awakened at two-thirty-five by the phone.

"Mrs. Price?" a voice asked.

"Yes, this is Diane Price."

"I'm Officer Johnson. Do you have a son named Michael?"

"Yes, I do. Is he all right?" Diane sat up and began to search for a pen and piece of paper in case she needed to take notes.

"I'm afraid there's been an accident," the police officer said. "No one was hurt, but both the driver and your son have been drinking. He's here at the station."

"I'll be right there." Diane dressed and drove to the police station. You knew this would happen someday, a voice inside told her. It was only a matter of time. Just like his father.

"No, he's not," she shouted to no one in particular. "He's a good kid, he is. Teenage boys always test the limits. It's just part of growing up," she reassured herself.

At the station the arresting officer pulled her aside to talk to her before releasing Michael.

"Your son is very lucky," he said. "He could easily have been hurt, but he got away with just a few bruises. But what's worse is that we have word that there were harder drugs at the party. Fortunately for your son and his buddy, nothing was found in their car. They may not be so lucky next time. I thought you should know."

"Are you saying my son is into drugs?" Diane could not believe what she was hearing.

"I'm saying the crowd he is hanging with is suspected of drug use."

"I see. Thank you, officer. I'll talk to Michael."

On the drive home, Diane and Michael spoke no more than a few sentences, at her insistence.

"Mom, I can explain," Michael told her, his face turned toward the passenger window.

"I don't want to discuss it, Michael. For your own good I suggest you keep your mouth shut before I say something we both will regret. I'm way too angry to be rational right now."

They rode in silence, her head a flurry of words, none making any sense. The phrase, "What did I do wrong?" kept repeating endlessly in her head and even in her sleep when she finally managed to get some that night. Happy New Year. What a way to start the year.

"Sorry to hear about Michael," one of her salespeople greeted Diane after the holidays when Diane entered the boutique dress shop that she owned. News sure travels fast, she thought.

"Yeah. It's time to mark down some of those holiday dresses." Diane put her employee to work while she escaped to the office to take care of paperwork. She knew the other employees were probably discussing her son too, but at least she didn't have to hear it.

Diane had achieved some small success as a retailer. After the divorce she had started working at a local dress shop while attending school at night. She had learned all aspects of the business and managed to get a loan to buy the shop when the owner retired. She enjoyed the independence of being her own boss and had managed to make a good living, but now the offer to be bought out by a large chain seemed even more appealing.

"You could stay on as store manager. In fact, you might even be put in charge of a larger store in another city. There's room for growth in our company," one of the chain's corporate vice presidents told her while discussing a buyout offer.

Diane didn't know what she wanted to do. She was too young to retire, too old to begin all over again, wasn't she? She stared off into space, no longer even pretending to be working. It sounded good, this opportunity. A new job, new city, new life. What did she have to keep her here?

Diane rolled over the next morning and hit the snooze on her alarm clock. She did not want to get up. Why was it so hard to get up every morning? Certainly if she had been going to sink into a depression the time to do it would have been when her husband had left her with two small kids to take care of eleven years ago. But then she had had to keep going for their sakes. She couldn't afford the luxury of a breakdown. She couldn't afford to lie in bed day after day, hour after hour in a state of depression. Someone had to cook the meals, wash the clothes, clean the house, help with homework. Someone had to be gainfully employed to pay the bills. That someone was her. She couldn't afford a depression then. Could she now?

One child, Adrian, was grown up and on her own; the other, Michael, was close to being there. Soon Diane would be free to do all the things she had always wanted. Why didn't she feel free? She felt trapped in a nowhere job in a nowhere community in the upper Midwest where the only single men were either twice her age, or half her age, or spent their free time in their trucks, hunting and drinking and talking about hunting and drinking with their buddies. Not a very appealing prospect. She had stayed for the sake of the kids, but now it was no longer a good situation for her son. Perhaps now she was free to leave.

After the third time hitting the snooze, she dragged herself out of bed and into the bathroom. Coffee, she needed coffee. She followed the smell of freshly brewed coffee coming from her kitchen. That programmable coffeemaker had been worth every penny, would have been worth twice what she had paid. That first cup tasted so delicious she craved another. She poured her second cup then went back to her seat at the kitchen table where she could look out the window and watch over her yard. There were fresh tracks on the snow from visiting deer and rabbits. There were matching tracks in her brain, etchings that were the marks of her life, haphazard as her life journey had been so far.

The dark tendrils of depression were creeping nearer and nearer, waiting to sink into her brain like an inoperable tumor. She had to do something to keep it from getting a stranglehold on her.

She picked up the phone and called her friend Marge and arranged to meet her for lunch then quieted her mind enough to go to work.

Marge greeted her with a hug. "So sorry to hear about Michael's run-in with the law." News does travel fast, Diane thought again.

"That's just a part of it, Marge. That's not what I wanted to talk about," Diane paused before continuing. "Marge, I'm thinking about selling out."

"The store?"

"Yes, I've gotten a good offer. Not only that, the company that wants to buy the store has offered to place me in management in one of their other stores, maybe a larger store in a larger city."

"But what about Michael?"

"I don't think Michael's in much of a place to bargain one way or another. He's mixed up with a bad crowd. Maybe a move would be just what he needs, a new start, new friends."

"Or worse friends and worse trouble in a bigger city."

"I've thought about that, but this isn't just about Michael. It's about me too. Me. When is there going to be time for me? I'm over forty years old and what do I have to show for it? A divorce, a small-town store, and a son that I have to pick up at the police station." Diane shook her head and sighed so loud that it surprised both her and Marge.

"Have you talked with anyone else about this?" Marge questioned.

"Not yet."

"How about someone at church?"

"That won't do any good. I've tried and tried. I've talked to the minister about Michael. I've tried to get him into some activities at church, tried to get him to join the youth group. And I've prayed. How I've prayed. I know Michael needs male guidance in his life, someone to help him know what it is to be a man. I've prayed that God would send someone, some man, a big brother or a teacher or a coach. Someone who would take an interest in Michael. Someone that Michael could relate to. I've prayed and I've tried. I've looked for men in the community willing to take Michael under their wing, and none have come forward. I'm tired of praying. I'm tired of my life. I want a life too." Diane shook her head, fighting the tears that threatened to fall from her eyes. She grabbed a Kleenex from her purse and blew her nose.

"I'm worried about you, Diane. You don't seem like yourself."

Diane picked at the lettuce on her plate before answering. "Sometimes I'm still so angry, angry at Tom for leaving, even though I know my life got better once he left. I get angry at myself for having married him in the first place, and angry at the kids and all of their demands, even though I know they were my saving grace back when Tom left. They were my reason for living. And I'm angry at God for bringing me to this place and abandoning me."

Diane paused to take a breath before continuing. "All my life I tried to be the good daughter and good wife. I stayed with Tom even when others advised me to leave because I thought that was what God wanted me to do. I stayed in this town because I thought that was what God wanted me to do. It's different now. My kids don't need me like they used to. Now I feel so alone. I have to have something else in my life."

Marge reached out for Diane's hand. "Diane, I had no idea. I'm so sorry. I haven't been the best friend."

"No, Marge, you've been a good friend. Now I've hurt you when I never meant to. It's me. I hate to say it, but it truly is all about me, not you. You've been great. I'm sorry."

"What about Adrian?"

"She's off at college, off in her own world, starting a new life of her own. What would she care? She hardly comes home for the holidays. And depending on where I move, I may be closer to her. Maybe we could grow closer."

"Sounds like you've already made up your mind."

Diane paused and stirred the bowl of soup that was growing cold in front of her, pushed it aside, and took a bite of salad. "Maybe I have. I just have to take the steps to make it happen."

"Well, if anyone deserves a second chance, it's you, Diane," Marge said. "I've seen how you've worked the past eleven years since Tom left. Raising the kids on your own, struggling to make ends meet, to better yourself and provide a life for your children. You've always put the kids first. Maybe that was a mistake. Maybe if you would have allowed yourself more of a social life you could have found someone. . ."

"Marge, I don't need to hear this again."

"But maybe, Diane, maybe then there would have been a man in Michael's life and your own, to help you."

"Look, I'm not going to lie and say I'm not interested, but . . . you know what my life has been like. I guess I just figured if it was meant to be, it would happen, and if not, it wouldn't happen. But that's another reason for a move. I'm not getting any younger. I don't want to live my life alone, but my chances of meeting someone here does not appear to be that good."

"There's Doug, the church organist."

"Marge, I've told you before. I'm not looking to be fixed up with anyone."

"But he's cute."

"And he knows it. Besides, he's not interested in me."

"How do you know if you don't ask?"

Diane laughed. "Haven't we done this before?"

"It's good to see you laugh, Diane. You need more laughter in your life."

"And good friends. I'm going to miss you."

"You're not getting rid of me. I expect you to go some place exotic so I'll have an excuse to travel. Who knows, maybe I'll meet someone exciting and leave my John behind."

They laughed at this, another joke shared between them. Despite her complaints at times, Diane knew Marge and John were definitely a "couple" in the truest sense. In fact, that made it easier for Diane to joke, for the likelihood of Marge ever leaving John was nonexistent. The two women finished their lunches, chatted about common acquaintances, then hugged again as they left.

"I'll miss you if you leave," Marge said.

"When I leave," Diane corrected her.

"Okay, when. Just make sure it's not too soon. You've got to give me some time to get used to the idea."

Diane felt both better afterward and more fearful. It seemed the die had been cast.

Chapter 2

Diane looked at the boutique's window display and decided to move a mannequin and add a scarf for a splash of color.

"No, that's not what I had in mind," she told the young window dresser. "It's dull and lifeless."

"What do you expect? They are dummies," Diane heard a familiar voice and turned to see her best friend.

"Marge, is it time for lunch already?" Diane stepped down from the platform that held the mannequins in varying stages of dress. "See what you can do to liven this up," Diane instructed the window dresser before leaving.

"Pinch me," Diane said at lunch. "I can't believe it's real."

"You look good," Marge smiled at her. "It's hard to believe that it's only been a year since you were back in your own store in Stanton."

"Do you believe it? Three moves in one year. Me, who never lived anywhere but Stanton. Whose only move had been from my parents' home to the home my kids grew up in. Me, Diane Price, on the management track."

The last year had been a whirlwind of activity and movement. Three moves, three different cities, each a little bigger than the one before. She was being moved from one store to another in preparation for . . . Diane wasn't sure what. A bigger and better store? Better wages, more opportunities? Diane wasn't sure what she wanted, but after over forty years in one city, she went along for the ride and was enjoying it.

With each move she left behind yet another layer of her former self, the self she had been. Here she was no longer George and Julie's daughter, Tom's ex-wife, Adrian and Michael's mother, store owner. She had left all that behind in the town that had defined her in so many ways. Not that she had stopped being all of those things, especially not being a mother. But at the store, she was just another employee, first a manager in training, then an assistant manager. It just so happened that she had a teenage son in tow with every move, but that was peripheral to her reality on the job.

Diane liked the new-found freedom from so many roles and the expectations that went along with it. It was a little scary, but it was also almost intoxicating. She was coming into her own even though she wasn't sure yet what that would be. It scared her at times as vestiges of her old self called back to her. Still it was exciting. If only Michael also experienced it that way.

As much as Diane was enjoying her freedom, Michael was resisting the changes both of locale and within her. He had not wanted to leave his friends, especially not for his senior year. Diane understood this and had considered working out with her parents for Michael to remain with them and finish out his senior year. However, his friends had not been the best influence on him. He had been in and out of trouble all through high school. Diane had hoped that maybe the move would be good for him, give him a fresh start in a fresh school, and allow him to make new friends, hopefully better ones. Diane had been wrong. At each new school he sought out the worst in the student population. those involved with drugs and gangs. The problems just got worse instead of better. Michael was exposed to greater opportunity for getting into trouble than he had had in his hometown.

But this wasn't about him, Diane told herself. This time it wasn't about him at all. Of course, Michael told her that too. He blamed her for his problems.

"It's all your fault, Mom. This wouldn't have happened if I had stayed home with my friends, if you hadn't taken this new job. I can't believe you are being so selfish."

Adrian had echoed her brother's sentiment too. "Mother, I can't believe you sold our house. You are being so selfish."

Diane told herself that it was "about me" now and finally doing something more with her life. She had devoted so much of her adult life to raising her two children, putting their needs before her own, just as she had done with their dad before he had left her. Codependency they had called it. Enabling. By putting others first she had enabled her former husband to be an alcoholic. She always knew she was to blame, knew he'd find some way to blame her for the fact that he drank. Isn't that how it always worked?

And now, of course, it was her fault her son was messed up. His dad had nothing to do with it. It was her fault because it was always her fault. So she was going to stop enabling, taking care of him and finally do something for herself. Maybe she should have waited one more year. After all what's a year in the wider scheme of things when you already have forty under your belt? A year for a teenager is a much bigger deal. But she had known she couldn't handle one more year there. She just had to get out.

If she hadn't left then, she had been afraid she would have found herself trapped forever. She would have grown old and bitter trapped in the same town with the same people. She had had to get away, even if only for a while. Even if she returned later. She had had to get away while she could. Years of neglect and putting everyone else's needs before her own had pushed her to the breaking point.

"Yes, I am being selfish and about time, isn't it? Isn't it about time I had a life of my own?" Diane bit her tongue lest she rattle off words she didn't really mean, words that would be hard to take back. She didn't want to lose her children, just gain her life.

Adrian would come around. Diane knew that. She was upset that Diane had sold their house. "Where am I supposed to go for the holidays and breaks?"

"You can stay with me like always. Isn't it the people who make the home?"

"Complete strangers are living in my home. That's the only home I've ever known."

"And you will know more. Many more."

"I don't want more. I want that one."

"I know you do, but it's not my home anymore and you just have to accept that."

Diane ended the discussion. She knew it wasn't going anywhere. Adrian had unwillingly joined her and Michael for Christmas in her two-bedroom apartment. Diane had done her best to make Christmas special, purchasing a tree from the corner lot a block away from her downtown apartment and decorating it single-handedly. Adrian made a point of being gloomy and moping to show her displeasure. It came as no surprise and something of a relief when she had announced she would be spending spring break with her friends.

Diane had compensated by throwing herself into her work. It was the one area of her life that was going well. She was making progress, showing potential. Here she got the positive feedback she had been lacking for so long.

The most recent move had been to a much larger store in a large metropolitan area as assistant manager. She liked the excitement of the big city, the theater and cultural opportunities. She also heard about the nightlife and had even had a few tentative dates, but dating wasn't high on her priorities right now. After so many years of caring for others, she was afraid of getting trapped into a relationship and the responsibilities that entailed.

"What do I want with a relationship right now?" she told Marge once the conversation turned to the inevitable subject. "I'm tired of cooking and cleaning for other people. I have enough to do with just taking care of myself. And then there's Michael."

"Yes, Michael . . . but where have you been, girl? Don't you know that men today actually know how to cook and share in the household chores?"

"You find me a man who can cook, and maybe I'll consider him."

"And besides, there's more to marriage than cooking and cleaning."

"Like what? After such a long dry spell, cooking and cleaning is all I know."

"Like romance. Wouldn't you like a little romance in your life?"

"What's romance got to do with marriage?"

"Precisely!" They both laughed.

"Who said romance had to lead to marriage? What about a little fun, adventure, and then see what develops?"

"I could stand a little romance, a little music, a little dancing, a little champagne," Diane admitted with a grin. "It wouldn't hurt. So where is the man to make all this happen?"

"You can make it happen yourself. Aren't there any attractive men your age where you work? Or how about customers?"

"Sure, the only male customers I get are either shopping for clothes for their wives or their mistresses. Either way I lose."

"Something will come up, if you're open to it. I'm sure of it. Are you open though?"

"I don't know. I guess I am. I think I am. I've been ready for years on one level, but then . . . I don't know. I guess I'm afraid of being hurt again."

"Aren't we all? But hurt is a part of life."

Maybe so, Diane thought to herself, but that doesn't make it any easier. And yes, she was afraid. Afraid she would choose wrong again, get involved with the wrong man. I'm better off single, she thought. No one to fuss over or to fuss over me, no one to answer to, she mused. I like that, she said to herself. Still the nights were so long and getting longer now that the kids were growing up and almost on their own. What would she do then?

"Hey, Diane, you there?"

"Yeah, I'm sorry." Diane shook herself out of her trance. "Lost in a fog, I guess."

"Aren't we all? Has something to do with 'the change' I hear," Marge told her. "I've got to go," she added, getting up from the table. 'Let me know how you are. And don't forget to leave a little room for romance."

"Yeah, I'll do that," Diane agreed, but she knew she was lying. If romance were going to find her, it would have to drag her kicking and screaming out from under her bed.

Chapter 3

Jake had wandered around New York for some time, staying in shelters, living on the street. He wanted to avoid anyone who had ever known him. Didn't want them to see him, not that they'd recognize him looking like he did. He had been saved countless times as he paid for his meals by attending services at the Rescue Mission. Who knows, maybe one of these times it might actually do some good, he thought. Didn't hurt anyway. He was searching—but for what, he wasn't sure.

As he spent long days and longer nights on the street, he recognized he was changing in some deep, profound way that he didn't understand. Perhaps it was the lack of sleep, the poor food, being exposed to the elements, the fear for his safety. Certainly all of these had a profound impact on anyone living this lifestyle over time, but the impact went beyond that. It was not a great alteration, but something was happening. Jake knew that. He was just biding his time, allowing it to happen.

It was no great revelation that told him it was time to move back to the Midwest. It just seemed like it was time. He wasn't exactly sure how he ended up behind the line serving soup rather than being served, but somehow he did. And then the next thing he knew he was working as a janitor at the Salvation Army and earning enough money to rent a small apartment. The people at the mission pointed at him as their success story, one guy they had managed to get off the street. He let them believe it. There was no harm in it. But he knew they hadn't gotten him off the street. He had been ready to get off the street and allowed it to happen. He told no one of his past. He didn't want to remember or be reminded, although he did think about his kids, wondered how they were doing and what they thought of him.

"Laura?" he called his ex-wife one day from a pay phone.

"Jake? Where are you?" Laura asked, with genuine concern in her voice.

"Doesn't matter, does it? How are you? How are the kids?"

"They're fine, Jake, no thanks to you. Where in God's name are you anyway?"

"I think we've got a bad connection, Laura. Give my love to the kids. Nice talking to you."

"Don't you hang up on me . . ." Laura screeched as Jake hung up the phone. He had heard that tone far too many times in the past.

"So much for reconnecting with my family," Jake thought. "Maybe I'll try again in a couple of months." He had thought about writing but was afraid a letter would be too easily tracked down. He was determined not to be found till he was ready to be found.

"I'm out of here," Michael announced one night after an especially long and trying day at work for Diane.

"And where are you going?"

"I don't know. Anywhere but here. You can't stop me."

That summer with Michael was proving to be the worst yet. He had done so poorly in school that he had not graduated. He seemed resistant to any suggestion of repeating his senior year. It was that or get his G.E.D. He had to do one or the other. At least that was what Diane had thought. Michael had different plans, plans that didn't involve his mother.

"Look, I'm very tired, Michael," Diane told her son, the weariness settling in her voice and shoulders. "I haven't had anything to eat yet. Can't this wait till morning?"

"Sure, Mom, whatever you say. It's always got to be on your schedule, your time frame, doesn't it?" Michael stated defiantly.

In the morning when Diane checked his bedroom, Michael was gone. Diane was frantic. She called in sick at work and then called the police.

"How old is he?" the officer on the phone asked.

"Seventeen, almost eighteen."

"How long has he been missing?"

"Just this morning. He was here last night but not in his bed this morning."

"Sorry, lady. That is not long enough to be considered a missing person. Call us back in a few days if he's still missing. I suggest you call around to his friends to see where he might be."

"But that's just it," Diane thought to herself as she replaced the receiver of the phone. "He doesn't have any friends here. At least none that I'm aware of. He hasn't lived here long enough to make any friends. Maybe he's gone back home."

She called the bus station to find out when the first bus for her
hometown departed. Not till nine-fifteen., she learned from the
reservation clerk.

"Did you see a tall, lanky teenager in the station, about six feet,
with sandy brown hair, hanging below his ears, seventeen years old?
Did he buy a ticket?"

"Why yes," the woman answered. "He's been waiting here
since I got here at seven. Why?"

"Please don't let him get on that bus."

"I'm sorry, ma'am. I can't prevent him from boarding."

"I'll be right there," Diane said, hanging up the phone and
grabbing her purse before dashing for the door.

She got to the station just as the bus for Stanton pulled up.
Michael wasn't there. She found him at the video arcade spending
his last quarter on video games to kill time. She slid alongside the
machine and watched her son quietly, not sure what to say, not
wanting to break his concentration.

Michael ignored her, pretending to be intent on the game, but
she could see his concentration had been broken as he missed an
easy shot and the game ended.

"What are you doing here?" he snapped.

"Shouldn't I be the one asking that?" she responded.

"I told you last night I was leaving."

"I thought we were going to talk about it in the morning."

"What's there to talk about? I'm going. You can't stop me."

"Maybe not, but can't we talk first? After all, I've been your
mother for the past seventeen years. What's one hour to talk with
me? Are you hungry?"

"Yeah."

"We can get something to eat. You can always catch a later
bus."

"What about your job?" he said, his face still intent on the video
game.

"I called in sick. What good are sick days if you never take
them? Besides, you are more important than my job."

"I find that hard to believe."

"Well, believe it or not, it's true, Michael. Come on. Time for
some breakfast."

"You aren't going to change my mind."

"So, what will it cost you then? Just a little time and at least you'll have a full stomach."

He appeared to be wavering then thought better of it. "Look, Mom. I know all of your tricks. They may have worked on me when I was eight, but not anymore. I'm out of here. I hate it here. There's nothing here for me. If I don't catch this bus, then I'll take a train. I'll hitchhike. I'll do anything but stay."

"You're right, Michael," Diane said. "I can't make you stay. You're too old for that. But I am asking you to talk to me before you go. Please talk to me."

"It's too late for that, Mom. There's nothing to talk about. I gotta go." Michael grabbed his backpack and walked to the bus that was boarding. Diane fought back the urge to run after him, crying, begging him to stay. She didn't want that to be his last memory of her before he left. She wanted to keep her dignity in tact as well as allow him some dignity.

"You will e-mail me, won't you?" she said to his departing back. She knew he wouldn't. He had never been one to write. He didn't turn back. She stood and watched the bus pull away. She couldn't see him. He sat on the far side of the bus from where she stood. Still, she raised her hand to wave. She stood for a long while in the same spot, long after the bus had departed. She was jostled at times by other passengers.

"Why don't you look out?" one man snarled at her after a particularly rough bump. Diane slowly walked out of the bus depot and out into the bright morning. The sun was shining, the sky was clear. It looked like it would be a beautiful summer day. Diane pulled her jacket more tightly around her, clutched her purse, and walked aimlessly on the street till she came to a park bench. She sat down and stared off into space.

"You look like you could use a cup of coffee," a male voice broke into her thoughts.

"What?" she said.

"I said, you look like you could use a cup of coffee." The voice said again and handed her a steaming Styrofoam cup with a lid on it. "I hope you like it black."

"Oh, that's fine. I mean, no, thank you. I don't want it," Diane started to refuse the cup.

"Hey, just a sip or two. Besides, I hate to drink alone. Mind if I sit down?"

"No, er, yes, I do mind," Diane stammered. The man sat down anyway.

"I don't mean to be rude," he told Diane, "but I've been watching you sit here for some time. You looked like you needed a friend, so I thought a cup of coffee wouldn't hurt."

"I, I . . ." Diane started to put up a fight. She wanted to tell him to leave, or at least she wanted to leave, but she couldn't get the words out nor could she move her legs. Instead she found herself accepting the cup of coffee, wrapping her fingers around the warm Styrofoam, and taking a tentative sip.

"Thank you," she said, but didn't sip any more as she stared off into space.

"Care to talk about it?" the man quietly asked.

"No, yes, I don't know." Her brain just didn't seem to be functioning. It was so overloaded. She couldn't think, couldn't see straight. Still, the warmth of the coffee cup was something she could hold onto. It seemed to be all that was real right now. She took another sip.

Jake sat quietly alongside of her, biding his time. He'd seen that look so many times before. He'd seen it on women he had met living on the street. A vacant stare that masked a deep sorrow. But this one was different. She was obviously not a street person. She didn't have the street look about her. She was dressed too well and even if not wearing makeup, her hair had been combed. But she had the distracted stare some street women had. It was a stare that hid so much. It wasn't a permanent fixture on her face. He knew that. It hadn't become affixed permanently by years of street living, but it was there. Something in him wanted to find out what was behind the stare while he still could. He knew enough to give her space. He watched as she took another tentative sip of the coffee. Then she looked over at him.

"Oh, I'm sorry. Did I even say thank you?" she asked.

"You just did. Care to talk about it?" he repeated gently.

Diane slowly looked over at this man. He seemed harmless, but you never could tell. He looked older than her, but not by much. He was dressed more like a street person than a businessman, but his voice was kind. He appeared to be washed and clean-shaven. He didn't smell of the street like many homeless. What was she even thinking, she asked herself? She should, if not run, at least politely get up, thank him for the coffee, and leave. But her feet didn't want to cooperate. Besides, she had as much right to be here as he did. More, because she was here first. She wasn't going to let him scare her off. And what harm was there in talking to someone in broad daylight? He wasn't going to pull her kicking and screaming across the busy, crowded sidewalk and the even busier street to some back alley somewhere. Maybe she could wait him out. Maybe he would leave.

Jake's years on the street had taught him patience, so he waited. He had all the time in the world right now, and he was willing to wait.

He laughed at a couple of ducks splashing in the pond. Diane turned in the direction he was looking. A toddler was running after other ducks on the lawn and laughing as they squawked away. Diane smiled. She enjoyed the sense of gentle camaraderie.

"It's nice and peaceful here," Jake commented.

"Yes, it is. This is the first time I've really been here."

"So what brings you here? A holiday?"

"No, I took a day off from work." This reminded her of the reason she wasn't at work. She stopped smiling.

"That bad?"

"Huh?"

"The work, that bad?"

"No, work is just great. It's the rest of my life that's a mess." Diane was surprised to hear herself say this. Still what was there to lose? She would probably never see this man again. They obviously didn't run in the same circles.

"Kids? Relationships?" Jake had noted that she did not wear a ring.

"Kids, or more precisely, son. He just ran away from home."

"How old is he?"

"Seventeen."

"Hard to stop them when they reach that age."

"Don't I know."

"Sometimes you just have to let them go."

"I know, it's just . . . I'm so tired of letting go, all the time letting go, of people and places, things. Isn't there anything in life that lasts? Don't answer. I already know the answer," Diane said. She knew the answer. Nothing lasts. Nothing lasts in this world. She knew it, but she hated it. "I just want something in my life, something more, something that means something, something that lasts. I just wish I made a difference. I want to think that somehow I made a difference. That the world is a better place because of me, not that it's worse . . ." Diane surprised herself at what came out and how vehemently she expressed her feelings.

Jake sat quietly and took all of this in, thinking before saying, "Here, come with me." Jake stood up, offered her his hand and pulled her up with him.

"Wait, I don't know you."

"It's okay. Come with me."

Diane felt pulled in two directions. There was no guarantee about her safety and she didn't know anything about this man. Yet, he had kind eyes, so she decided to go along with him. "I guess the day couldn't get much worse, could it?" she thought to herself.

"By the way, my name's Jake, and yours?"

"Diane."

"Diane, pleased to meet you," he said as he took hold of her hand.

"Where are we going?"

"You'll see. Just follow me."

Where Jake took Diane was the library. He pointed out street people he knew.

"It's a good place to go during the summer to avoid excessive heat and during the winter to avoid the cold. Usually the librarians are pretty tolerant as long as the street people don't make any noise and disturb the other patrons. Here, let's sit here for a minute."

They sat down on a couple of connected chairs in a reading section of the library. Off in a corner by herself Jake and Diane could see a young woman in her late twenties or thirties with long stringy blond hair just standing and staring off into space with a vacant look on her face.

"She appeared at the shelter I was helping at one day," Jake began to whisper the young woman's story. "Her name is Mary. I can't remember how she got there. Someone had let her off at our door, gently guiding her out of the car and walking her through the front door. Then she became our responsibility as they drove away.

"She stood inside the door, quiet and staring, long blond hair, round face, fair complexion. She stared off into space as if seeing nothing yet seeing everything. She quietly picked at what was set before her to eat, choosing only those items that appealed to her, sweets and breads mostly. She stood wherever you led her and only sat down when led to a chair and guided into it. She caused no problems and kept to herself, despite efforts of other residents to talk to her. Still for all of her show of being unaware of her surroundings, Mary was keenly aware of what was going on around her.

"In the morning she had to leave with the other guests. Guests were supposed to look for a permanent home during the day. Mary left with the others, walking with that far-off expression on her face. Somehow she always made it back to us, sometimes brought by other people, sometimes showing up on her own.

"One time I followed her, wondering what it was she did all day. How did she manage to avoid being hit by a car as she stepped out into the street, neither looking right or left? But she seemed to have a sense about her that told her when it was all right to walk. She never walked out right in front of traffic. Sometimes others helped her across the street. Other guests from the shelter who knew her would look out for her. She was quickly becoming known on the street, and the network was looking out for her to keep her safe.

"I followed her to the library where she stood for hours, it seemed, in one place, till I had to leave and get back to my other responsibilities. Sometimes she would speak, but very little.

"One day a knock was heard on the shelter door. Two men stood there—one young, the other old. Father and son. They were looking for a woman—daughter to one, sister to the other. Denise was her name. The shelter director and I told them we had no Denise staying here but invited them inside anyway.

"'What does she look like? Maybe we've seen her?'" the director and I asked. The description they gave was familiar. 'Mary!' The director and I looked at each other and said in unison.

"The father and son told the story of a talented young woman who had gone to the West Coast, got caught up in the drug culture, had a bad trip on LSD, and came back like this, a shell of her former self. They tried to care for her at home, but every now and then

Denise would walk away and show up in different cities until they found her and took her back home.

"I told them they could probably find her at the library. If not, she would be back here around four. They left for a while then returned at four to await her return. There was a glimmer of recognition as Mary walked through the door and saw her brother and father, and a look as if she were about to run. She didn't want to leave with them. Then the vacant stare returned, much to her father's dismay, and she allowed herself to be led back into the awaiting car, taken back home until she could run again.

"Now her father lets her come here during the day. Sometimes her father drops her off and picks her up, sometimes her brother," Jake concluded the story. "What time is it?" he asked, glancing at Diane's watch.

"A little after noon, why?"

"Let's get something to eat, then I have somewhere else to take you."

This time Diane went along more willingly. She was intrigued by this man and his stories. After grabbing a bite to eat from a street vendor, Jake took Diane to a local Baptist church. Diane and Jake watched from the back of the church as the people filed in—some alone, others in groups of two or three or more, clinging to each other, unsure of themselves in this new surroundings.

"What's happening?" Diane asked.

"A funeral for one of the sisters from the street," Jake explained.

She and Jake watched people file in—brothers and sisters from the streets, from the neighborhood, crack addicts, prostitutes, drug dealers, numbers runners—mixed in with relatives from the suburbs, workers from the neighborhood, store owners, cashiers, construction workers, waitresses. The mourners kept coming and coming till the main floor of the church sanctuary was filled. Then the crowd filled the balcony and the vestibule and overflowed onto the parking lot. The church was not big enough to hold all who had come to pay respects to this simple young woman.

She had been baptized in this church, had once lived in this area of town, but her folks had moved out to the suburbs shortly after her baptism to escape the crime of the city, Jake explained quietly to Diane. She had found her way back to the projects as a young

woman, falling prey to the lure of that most seductive of drugs—
crack. She had been someone's daughter and a mother herself,
leaving behind two children. Her own mama had not wanted the
funeral at her church in the suburbs, didn't want her friends to know
how far her baby had sunk. So the mother came back to the projects
and asked this favor of her former church—to bury her daughter who
had died, strangled in her apartment.

"Not everyone would have said yes to such a request," Jake
said, a tinge of sadness in his tone. "They only buried their own."

But this girl was their own, the senior pastor said, even if she
had not set foot in the church since her baptism. She was from the
neighborhood and thus one of their sheep. The church had expected
a small turnout, twenty or so at most. Instead, the senior pastor and
his associate waited and waited as the people kept coming, filling the
church to overflowing. The associate welcomed the brothers from
the street with a brotherly hug and shakedown, checking for
concealed weapons.

"Yo, Rev."

"Welcome, bro!"

Finally, the family was gathered along with extended family
from the street. The service began. Angela's mother and children sat
in the front pew. The "Amens" were subdued and sorrowful as the
pastor welcomed all to the service and led the opening prayer for
"our sister, Angela." When he invited those in attendance to speak,
one by one people began to come forward with their own testimony
of what this woman had meant to them.

"Angela was my big sister," said one mourner who looked
everyone in the eye as she gave her testimony. "Angela looked out
for me, kept me out of trouble. She told me, 'Don't you be hanging
out with those drug dealers. Don't you be fooled by their fancy cars
and fancy clothes.' I listened to her because I knew she cared about
me."

A man dressed in his work clothes from a construction site
came forward. "'I apologize for these clothes, but I had to leave my
job to come, and I have to go right back. But I came to tell you,
Angela saved my life. When I was a teenager like some of you, I
thought it was cool to sell drugs. But then I got hooked on cocaine,
and it wasn't so cool. I found myself in the gutter. Angela pulled me
out of the gutter. She told me to get my life in order, to get off of the

drugs. She helped me beat the habit. I'm drug free and alive today, thanks to Angela. That's all I wanted to say."

One by one the stories told were the same, of some kindness done, a kind word or deed. Angela had helped so many others but wasn't able to help herself.

Finally, when all had testified, the senior pastor glanced at his associate and both nodded. They knew no more needed to be said. All that was left was to take Angela to her final resting place. The funeral procession extended for blocks throughout the city, stopping traffic. Who was this person with such a long parade in attendance, those passing by asked? Some local dignitary or businessman? No, just Angela, a crack addict who had lived in the projects and was strangled at the age of thirty-three.

Diane felt subdued after listening to the testimonies and almost in awe. Angela had been a crack addict, and yet look at all the lives she had touched, Diane thought. She and Jake didn't go to the burial site. It was too far to walk.

"I have one more place to take you," Jake said. Diane didn't respond. They hopped the bus and sat in silence for a while. Across from them sat an odd couple. Two street people. The woman seemed to be in a daze.

"Yeah, oh, yeah," the female bus passenger would say in a spaced-out voice and little more. Sometimes she would break out into giggles.

"That's Jack and Susan," Jake whispered after the two departed from the bus. Jake told Diane their story.

Jack was a dirty old coot, Jake told Diane, with gaps where teeth used to be, a guy who always made sexist comments to rile up the female workers at the shelter.

"'I'm gonna find myself someone to cook me bacon and eggs every day,' Jack used to say. How the two of them got together, no one knows. Susan was quite a bit younger than Jack. She appeared so vulnerable. We all thought that Jack was just taking advantage of her, but instead he was taking care of her. He gave her shelter, sharing his apartment with her, and he looked out for her. 'Susan makes me bacon and eggs every morning,' he'd say."

Sometimes, Jake told Diane, Susan would just take off, perhaps fed up with something Jack had said or done. "Jack was lost without Susan and searched high and low throughout the streets. He didn't rest till he found her and brought her back home with him. You'd see them riding the bus together, Jack talking, Susan just giggling or staring off into space. And Jack would make bacon and eggs for Susan every morning, or so I've been told," Jake finished the story just as he and Diane reached their stop.

Diane was smiling as they got off the bus. "Where are we going now?"

"Just another place where I work." Jake led Diane across the street to a soup kitchen. She paused at the sight of the people lined up, waiting to get in.

"Come on. These are just some more of my friends," Jake said as he led her past the line to a basement door.

"Hi, Jake," a number of men in line said. The women eyed Diane suspiciously. Jake brought her in through the basement and into the kitchen that was bustling with volunteers preparing a meal, not just soup.

"How many jobs do you have?" Diane asked.

"Only one that pays. I'm the janitor at the Salvation Army. That's the one that pays. The rest I do just because," he shrugged then called out, "Gladys, I brought you another volunteer." A large white woman with her hair swept into a stern bun under her hairnet grunted at Jake then went back to the stove where she was stirring pots. She pulled out a tray of biscuits, barked out a few orders, and ignored Diane.

"Don't worry about her," Jake assured Diane, giving her an apron and leading her out of the kitchen to the serving area. Soon Diane was ladling beef stew onto biscuits for the line that came in once the door was opened. Jake moved easily among the people, assisting wherever needed, bussing tables, chatting with folks. Diane found herself following him mentally around the room in between serving people. She could barely keep her eyes off him, he intrigued her so. Stripped to his t-shirt, Jake walked around the room unaware that Diane was eying the muscles that rippled his arms and chest. She realized he was possibly younger than she had first thought. Despite his lifestyle, Jake seemed to be aging well, Diane mused. There were flecks of gray in his brown hair. His face was somewhat weathered and wrinkled from the sun. It was not a young face, but not too old either. His blue eyes sparkled as he joked with the guests of the soup kitchen.

A couple of times Jake caught Diane watching him. She turned her eyes away in embarrassment. What was she doing? She should be focused on the people in front of her, serving each one graciously, attentively. Instead she was sneaking furtive glances at a man she barely knew, whom she had just met. Could this day get any crazier?

"Pay attention to what you're doing," Gladys snapped at her when she came out with a new pan of stew.

The elderly black woman by Diane's side who was placing biscuits on plates reassured her. "Don't worry about her. She's all bark, some bite, but she won't as long as Jake's around. He's some man, isn't he, dear?" She had seen Diane watching Jake.

Diane watched as Jake asked a young man to step out of line. With their backs to everyone, the man turned over a large knife to Jake who placed it somewhere in the kitchen.

"He's our best security," the elderly woman boasted. "I've been in some soup kitchens where they actually have a police officer standing guard over the people to make sure there are no fights. Jake put an end to that. He treats everybody with respect and insists on the same in return. He doesn't hide behind the counter and serve the people like some. He gets out there and mingles with them. They know him by name and he knows them. That's the best security, not a gun and a wall of fear."

"Does he run this place?" Diane asked.

"No, but he might as well. He does everything but. He says he doesn't want the responsibility or the hassles. Here, try some of Gladys' stew," Diane's neighbor said as the line finally came to an end. Diane sat down with the other volunteers for a bowl of stew before cleaning up. As the volunteers finished washing the last dish, Jake came over and took Diane by the hand.

"Sorry, Esther," he said to the black woman. "I hate to take such a good worker away, but I'm afraid I must if we're to catch the next bus."

"That's all right, child. We're almost done anyway," Esther said with a smile. "Come back any time, dear," she told Diane. Gladys merely grunted.

Diane was very quiet as she and Jake rode the bus together back to the bus station where she had left her car. Finally, she turned to him and said, "Who are you?"

"Jake, I told you. Jake Alexander."

"No, really, who are you? You didn't always do this, this thing that you're doing now. You didn't always live on the street or work with the homeless. Who are you? Who were you? I want to know."

"And what if I had lived on the street all of my adult life, would it make a difference?"

"I don't know," Diane said hesitantly.

Jake laughed, "That's for another time. I think you've had enough for one day."

"But will there be another time?" Diane asked tentatively, a bit of hope creeping into her question.

"That's up to you. You know how to find me. Goodnight, Ms. Diane. I hope you had a good day. I hope you forgive me for intruding on your solitude this morning." Jake took Diane's hand, pressed it lightly, then left. Diane was both relieved and dismayed that he hadn't kissed her, hadn't even tried.

Why was she thinking about kisses? What was she thinking? How could she have spent the day with a complete stranger? At least she hadn't given him her full name or phone number. At least he couldn't track her down even if he wanted to. She never had to see him again if she didn't want to, but she knew she wanted to. She wanted to see him again.

How foolish of me, she thought. I must be getting senile. I guess I've been too long between dates, too long without romance that I would jump so quickly at this possibility. Thank God, he doesn't have my phone number. Damn, why didn't he ask me for my phone number? Thank God, he didn't ask. Curses that he didn't. It'll all look different in the morning, Diane assured herself. Tomorrow will be a new day. I'll be able to put all of this behind me. I can forget about it. Besides, there's Michael to worry about, and work. As long as I can stay busy worrying about Michael and work, I won't be able to waste my time on this man I hardly know. Yes, Michael. I can't believe I've hardly thought about him all day.

These thoughts kept running through Diane's head as she drove back to her now empty apartment. No messages, she thought as she walked in and the phone message light wasn't blinking. Thank you, God. Once her parents realize Michael is back in town, they'll be on the phone to her. They must not know yet. At least I can have this much of a break. She picked up her cat as the hungry feline rubbed around her legs.

"Looks like it's just you and me, kid," Diane said to the cat. She carried the cat into the kitchen then sat the meowing fur ball on the counter as Diane prepared the cat's evening meal.

"There you go, Samantha," Diane said as she placed the food in a bowl on the kitchen floor. Just you and me and my thoughts to occupy my time, Diane muttered as she looked through the newspaper then prepared for bed. Just let me get through the night. Let me put today behind me and get on with my life. Time enough tomorrow to worry about today.

Chapter 4

She was wakened by the simultaneous ringing of her phone and her alarm. She shut off the alarm and reached for the phone, knowing without asking who it was.

"Hi, Mom," she said groggily.

"Diane, did you know Michael is back in town?"

"News travels fast. I know he took the bus yesterday morning. Did you see him?" Diane sat up in bed, shaking the sleep from her tired body.

"No, but Charlotte said she saw him last night with that no-good friend of his, Jimmy Page. I told her it couldn't be him, but then Eleanor said she saw him too." Eleanor was their neighbor. "What are you going to do about it?"

"Right now I'm going to take a shower and get ready for work."

"You can't let him stay here by himself." She could hear the underlying message in her mother's voice. She was not going to play that game.

"Mom, he's seventeen. I can't physically drag him home. I can't keep him tied up once I get him here either. At least there he has friends."

"Losers all of them. They'll end to no good, and they'll drag Michael down with them."

"Mom, if you see him, tell him I love him and to give me a call, collect, anytime, okay. I've got to go now. Love you." Diane hung up the phone. At least now she knew where he was and who he was with. It was not the best situation but it was better than being on the streets here. Streets. Jake. Street people. Did she dream it all? If so, what a strange dream. So strange. One minute she was sitting in the park not knowing what to do, the next she was being escorted through parts of town she had never seen by this man she had only just met. Strange. She had seen him in her dreams. Yesterday was like a dream. But today is reality. Time to get to work. That was real.

Diane was distracted all that day at work. So much so that the store manager asked her if something was wrong.

"Are you okay?" she asked thinking maybe she needed an additional day off. One of the other supervisors in the management track also noticed something was wrong. As an assistant manager who was looking to be manager someday, she was directly accountable to the store manager for her daily work, but was also under scrutiny of the higher ups in charge of training and placement of personnel. John Truscott seemed to be taking more than a passing interest in her career advancement.

"You seem distracted today. Is something wrong? Trouble at home?" he asked.

"No, well, yes. My son moved out yesterday." She knew she was taking a risk telling him this. Management types were not supposed to let family problems interfere with their work. However this seemed much safer than saying, "I met this man yesterday."

"How about we talk about it over drinks tonight, after work?"

"Oh, well, yes, okay. That sounds good." Diane was taken aback by the question. He seemed genuinely interested. What would a few drinks hurt? And perhaps it might help. He was mature, attractive and single, she believed. There was no wedding ring on his finger. But, of course, this was only business. He was just interested in her because of business, wasn't that right?"

Drinks were pleasant. She talked a little about Michael and Adrian and her life. He told her about himself. He was a widower whose kids were now adults, living on their own.

"That about sums it up, the story of my life. Sarah died a few years ago, just when we were looking at our 'golden years', whatever that means. The kids were out of the house and settled, we were making plans to travel, take some of those vacation days that had been piling up, when the heart attack took her. It was completely unexpected. She had always been in good health."

"I'm so sorry," Diane responded, reaching across the table to take his hand.

"Yes, well, that was then, life goes on." He had been surprised by the tears that were so close to the surface. "God never gives us more than we can handle, right?" he said with a wry smile. "Enough sad stories, would you like to go to the theater with me this weekend?"

"Yes, I would," Diane smiled into his grey eyes, still holding his hand.

"Then it's a date," John said, rising from the table. Diane found herself comparing John to Jake. His hands had none of the callouses of hard, physical labor but were strong none-the-less. His hair was dark, clearly dyed. She could see signs of grey at the roots. He was slender, without Jake's rugged good looks. He appeared to be in good shape for his years. She suspected he worked out, though it was hard to detect under his suit. It was evident he took good care of his appearance. He was a little shorter than Jake, yet still rose a few inches above her, the perfect height for a dancing partner, she thought.

What better way to forget about one man, than by becoming involved with another, right? But what was there to forget about this mystery man, Jake? One day with a complete stranger. She could forget him easily enough. She didn't know John that well either, but she had seen him enough at work and heard enough through the office rumor mill to believe he was worth her time. He was ten years her senior, well established and respected. She could easily convince herself to forget Jake for John. After so many years, to actually have two men in her life?! What a nice dilemma.

"So tell me more about this mystery man, Jake," Marge said during their monthly lunch date.

"What is there to tell? I spent one day with him. Nothing more. He didn't even ask me for my phone number. He was just coming to my rescue like he does for all those street people he knows. He saw I was in distress and tried to help me. Big deal. Nothing more."

"Hmmm, if you say so. And what about this John?"

"John, oh, I like John. He's nice to me. He's stable and reliable, everything Tom wasn't. It's a nice change . . ." The theater date had gone well and they had since had several more dinner dates.

"But . . . Come on, Diane, say it."

"Well, all right. He's a little dull. But dull is nice. I had plenty of excitement with Tom."

"But that was years ago. And it wasn't positive excitement."

"It was at first. Tom knew how to show you a good time. He was charming. He swept me off my feet. It wasn't till later, once we were married that I saw the other side of him. His irresponsibility. How immature he was. His drinking. I had been blind to all of that, blinded by his charm."

"Kind of like this Jake character. He sounds awfully charming to me."

"Yes, in his own way, he was. Oh, I don't know," Diane frowned down at her plate. "I don't know. I don't know if I can trust my judgment where men are concerned. I fell so hard for Tom and look what happened."

"Yes, but you were just a kid in high school then. Now you're an adult who's weathered many a storm."

"I still feel like that kid where men are concerned. I feel like I don't know anything more now than I did back then. Maybe that's the real reason why I haven't dated all these years. The kids were a convenient excuse not to get involved, not to get hurt."

"And now, that excuse is gone."

"I know. No more excuses. Anyway, John is solid and dependable. I know what to expect from him. I know where I stand."

Marge affected a yawn, "Boring," she said.

"So what's wrong with boring?"

"Nothing, if that's what you've been waiting for all this time, if that's what you want. You don't have to marry this guy, Jake, or any man right now. The least you should do is play the field a little. Give it a chance. Don't be so quick to settle into a relationship. Besides, isn't there a policy against dating your supervisor?"

"Just your immediate supervisor. John isn't my supervisor. He's just 'higher up' in management than me."

"You can date them both. Nothing wrong with that."

"So you're saying I should look this Jake up?"

"You said it, not me. What do you have to lose? A couple of hours of your time. So you get to know someone new. Maybe it'll be more than a passing acquaintance, maybe not. What'll it hurt?"

Good question, Diane thought to herself then pushed the thought to the back of her mind where she could take it out later. Marge filled her in on all that was happening in her hometown.

"Have you seen Michael?" Diane asked.

"Yes, now and then. He seems to still be hanging out with the same crowd. He and Jimmy are sharing an apartment. We'll see how long that will last." Yes, Diane thought. She had already gotten emails requesting money for Michael's share of the expenses. She wrote cordial emails back each time, but always with the same answer, no. He wanted to live on his own, he needed to get a job and support himself. He was welcome back home but then he had to be going back to school or in some way support himself. She would help with school, but that was it. No money otherwise. Her parents had already loaned him some money despite her protests.

"We can't see our grandson thrown out into the street," they had responded to her protests.

"He has a home he can come to if he wants. He needs to learn to be responsible for himself and his actions." Her pleas fell on deaf ears as they continued to help him out then complained to her about it. But they were a good four-hour drive away, six hours by bus. The distance made it somewhat easier. That and her job. She prayed for both her children each day, day and night, then left it to God as much as she could. Still she worried.

"More trouble with Michael?" John asked as he joined her for dinner that night.

"No more than the usual. You know, do you mind if we skip dinner tonight? I'm not feeling too well. I think I'd like to just go home, open a can of soup, then go to bed."

"Is there anything I can do? I can work a mean can opener," he offered.

"No. I'd rather be alone," she asserted. Gracious as always, John escorted her to her car.

"You up to driving?" he asked.

"Sure, no problem. I'm probably just tired. Goodnight." She got in the car and found herself aimlessly driving through town. She stopped at the park, got out and walked around as if hoping to run into Jake. But she knew he would probably be at the soup kitchen right now. Sitting on a bench by the fountain were Jack and Susan. She smiled as she walked by but didn't say hello. After all, they don't know her. She pulled her jacket around her as the sun sank further behind the building. She realized how foolish she was being. This was not the place for a lone woman at night. She got back into her car and decided to drive to the soup kitchen. She watched from her car as volunteers left, hoping to catch Jake on his way home. When Esther came out she called to her.

"Esther, Esther, over here."

Esther looked around then saw Diane calling from her car. She walked hesitantly towards the vehicle until she recognized Diane. "Why it's you, child. Why haven't you come back?"

"I was wondering, is Jake around?" Diane avoided her question by asking another question.

"Sure is. He's mopping floors. You want me to get him for you?"

"That's okay. I'll go in myself." Diane took a quick look around, wondered about the safety of her car, but decided to go ahead. Esther escorted her to the basement door.

"You'll have to knock real loud. It's locked for the night. Only Jake and a few volunteers left inside." Just as they started to knock the door opened and the remaining volunteers came out.

"Someone to see Jake," Esther said as they walked into the building.

"He's in the dining hall, last I saw him," a gentleman remarked as he left.

"Jake," Esther called through the darkened kitchen. Lights were still on in the dining room. Jake was stacking chairs on the table in preparation for mopping. "Someone here to see you," Esther pushed Diane forward. "I've got to get home. See you tomorrow, Jake."

Jake squinted into the darkened kitchen. "Is there something I can help you with?" he called into the shadows until Diane stepped forward. "Oh, it's you. Diane, right?"

"Yes, Diane." Diane felt extremely foolish. "You said I knew where to find you so I found you."

"Just a minute. I just have to finish mopping this floor. Then we can go. You in a hurry?"

"No, I guess I can wait."

"Great." Diane watched as Jake finished cleaning up. She walked aimlessly around the tables. "You do this every night?" she asked.

"Just about. I help out here, and at the Salvation Army as janitor."

"Oh," Diane said.

"It's not a lot, but it pays the bills. I don't need a lot. This way I have time for the really important things in life."

"Such as?"

"Such as spending the day with charming women who look like they need someone to talk to," he paused in his work to smile directly at her. He wrung out the mop, dumped the bucket and washed off his hands.

"There, that's enough for tonight. Let's get out of here."

"Where are we going?"

"You want some coffee? How about something to eat? Come on. I know a great diner. It's within walking distance, too." Diane followed along. Now that she had found him she didn't know what to say.

"So how is your son?" he asked as they walked slowly along the sidewalk.

"You remembered."

"Sure. I don't just pick up every woman I see on the street."

"I didn't know, I mean, you didn't call or anything . . ."

"No phone number. Besides I figured if you wanted to see me, you knew how to find me. And I was right, wasn't I?"

"Yes, I found you."

"I'm glad you did. Here's the diner." He held open the door for her.

"Hey, Jake. Coffee?" the cook behind the counter called out.

"Sure. And one for my friend here."

"Could you make that decaf? I don't want to be up all night."

"Sure thing lady. Charlene, two coffees, leaded and unleaded," he called to the waitress sitting at the end of the counter.

"Get it yourself. I'm on my break. I still got five minutes."

"Oh, all right." He wiped his hands on his apron then walked around the counter with two coffee cups. "Charlene will be right with you. So how are you tonight?"

"Just fine. How about breakfast?" Jake asked Diane. "Eddie makes the best breakfast. Then you won't have to eat when you get up tomorrow."

"Sounds good to me," Diane said realizing how hungry she was.

"I'll have the ham and eggs. You know how I like it," Jake told the cook.

"I'll have that too, eggs over easy," Diane said.

"Sure thing, Jake. I'll tell that lazy Charlene once she gets off break." He wandered back to the counter and threw some slabs of ham on the grill.

"So how have you been?" Jake asked. "And you haven't told me about your son yet."

"He's okay, I guess. He's got an apartment with a friend. I guess he's keeping out of trouble. He only e-mails to ask for money."

"Sounds pretty typical to me."

"But what about you? What have you been doing?"

"Pretty much the same as I've been doing. Working at the soup kitchen and Salvation Army."

"Here's your breakfast, Jake," Charlene sat the platters of food in front of them then refilled their coffee cups. "Anything else?"

"No, we're fine, thank you," Jake said.

"Is there anybody who doesn't know you?" Diane asked.

"Not around here I guess. I'm pretty much a fixture."

"How long have you been here?"

"Oh, a little over a year or so. Two years ago New Years, I was in Times Square watching the New Year come in with a bunch of people I didn't know. That was when I decided it was time to come back to the Midwest."

"You from here originally?"

"No, not here. I didn't want to go that far west. I was just tired of New York. So I came here and found myself a niche."

"But what did you do before that? Certainly you haven't always been a janitor or living on the street."

"I was on a street, just another street. Not all that different from any other street, just the people dress better and think that they're better, but they are not. I like the people on this street much better. They're more real, less phony. You know where you stand with them. I like it here. But what about you? What brought you here?"

"Work. A job. I'm a manager-in-training at Klein's department store. Right now I'm assistant manager. After a year or so I'll get to be manager in another store."

"So you'll be moving then?"

"Yes. This is my third move since I started with Klein's. I used to own a dress shop in my hometown. Right about the same time that you decided to leave New York, Klein's offered to buy me out and put me into management. I was ready for a change so I said yes."

"And here you are."

"Yes, here I am."

"So, are you happy?"

"Happy? I guess so. Maybe as happy as I've ever been. I don't know. What is happiness anyway? I'm not sure I know what happiness is."

"You didn't look too happy when I saw you on that park bench. I looked at you and thought, what does an attractive well-dressed woman like that have going on in her life to look so lost? That's why I decided to take a chance and talk to you. You seem to want more for your life."

"I do. I do want more. I'm just not sure what that more is. The offer at Klein's came at the right time, I guess. I was ready for a change so I took it. And now . . ."

"Here I am. Did I happen along at the right time?"

"I don't know. I don't know why you showed up in my life at the time you did. I don't know why I ended up on that park bench and why you just happened to be there. I don't know why I trusted you enough to spend the day with you rather than sending you away. And I don't know what I'm doing here, but here I am." Diane looked down at the remnants of egg yolk on her plate that she had failed to sop up with bread.

"Let's get out of here," Jake said as he laid down money for the bill. "Do you like jazz?"

"Yes, I do, but I better get home," Diane hesitated. "I've got work tomorrow."

"But the night is young, trust me. I'll get you home in plenty of time." He took her by the hand. "Thanks, Charlene. Eddie, excellent as usual," he said as he led Diane out of the diner.

Chapter 5

Diane was tired and yet elated that next day at work. They had listened to music until midnight. She had met more of Jake's friends. It was all a whirl in her head. They walked hand in hand down the street afterwards. She was a little nervous when she looked around at the shadows in corners, but with Jake she felt safe. He knew the streets and the people. She could trust him, she told herself. He escorted her to her car. Once again he didn't kiss her. She didn't know why. He held her hand in his and gently squeezed it then caressed her face. She had pulled away reluctantly. She wanted him to kiss her, and yet she didn't.

She felt so confused. Part of her felt like this was much too fast. Another part thought she'd be fifty before he kissed her. He seemed to like her. Why else would he have spent this time with her? He seemed to be enjoying himself and her company, but then maybe he was the type who enjoyed himself regardless of the company. She just happened to be the one who was around. And once again he didn't ask her for her phone number or address. She had no phone number for him. She hadn't asked. Why hadn't she asked? What a fool she was. All she had said was, "Will I see you again?"

"You know how to get a hold of me," he responded.

Once again the ball was left in her court. She wasn't sure what to do.

"I tried calling you last night. No one answered," John said later that day.

"I'm sorry. I just let the phone ring," she was not very good at lying and yet this one slipped off her tongue.

"How about dinner tonight? I'm going to have to be out of town all next week."

"Okay," she agreed. After all it was Friday. She could sleep in tomorrow. But what she really wanted was to say no, to find Jake wherever he was and spend the evening with him. But how would she find him over the weekend? And better to not seem too eager. "Sounds fine, John."

John took her out for dinner and dancing. She had been right - he was just the right height for a dance partner. He was not a shabby dancer and neither was she. They made quite the couple on the dance floor. She found herself laughing despite her tiredness. It was fun. Still she longed to get home to her apartment. Why, she didn't know. There wouldn't be any calls.

She resisted John's request for a night-cap in her apartment. She responded to his kiss but found part of her imagining it was Jake she was kissing. John, always the gentleman, graciously accepted her rebuff.

"I'm a patient man, Diane. If something's good, it's worth waiting for. You are worth waiting for," he told her. She was relieved to be home but also felt guilty. What a good man John was. How could she have lied to him? How could she go out with someone else? Still no promises had been made. No vows of love. She was a free agent, free to go out with whomever she pleased. Still she felt confused and guilty. Her heart thought of Jake. Her head told her to hold on to John. There was no agreement between the two.

Diane tried to sleep late that morning but found her brain was filled with far too many thoughts to allow her to rest. She got up, brewed a pot of coffee and sat in the window seat looking out across the street to the city below. Samantha climbed up and curled into her lap with a purr.

It was a small apartment, but nice. Two bedrooms, living area and kitchen combined. It was just right for her. Okay for her and Michael. Impossible when Adrian came to stay but those visits were short and infrequent. Besides with Michael moved out, Adrian could stay in his room. She could easily turn it into a guest room. She had a small balcony off her bedroom and this window seat. They were her favorite places. From here she could watch the world go by without her. She felt both a part of the life below and apart from it. It was a good space to be for her right now, finally, truly on her own without a lot of responsibilities. She had waited a long time for this. And now, not just one man in her life, but two. What more could a woman ask for? It was a good space, but not a permanent space. She knew that all along.

This was just a temporary stop along the way. She wasn't ready to put down roots just yet. And when she did, where would it be? And perhaps more important, with whom? Perhaps that was the attraction Jake held for her. He was unattached, at least as far as she could tell. He went where he wanted, did what he wanted, kind of like you, kitty, she thought. Independent. Why couldn't she be more like that? Not that she wanted to live on the street, but then where did he live? He must have an apartment somewhere. He did have a job, although how much it paid was most likely not much.

He didn't seem to want to have much yet he had all that he wanted and then some. Maybe he had some secret stash somewhere. Maybe he had millions in the bank and just lived this way because he wanted to. She had heard stories of rich street people. Of course their number was extremely small and it was extremely unlikely, still it was fun to fantasize. And, oh, Jake was well worth fantasizing about. Unlike John.

In comparison John was so dull and lifeless. She could imagine what life with John would be like. She would have all the comforts she would want. She would be taken care of. That might be a nice change, but was that really what she wanted? It would be nice to be taken care of after so many years of caring for others, but what was the catch? There always was a catch. Wouldn't she end up taking care of him? He was ten years older than her.

And then there was Jake. Life with him would be a mystery, wouldn't it? What does she really know about him? Very little. She didn't even know where he lived or what he did before. She knew he didn't live on the street all of his life. He didn't have the street look. He was too educated. She could tell he had a life before this one. A better one, or was it? If it had been better why would he have left it? There was only one way to find out. She had to see him again, but how? He had said she would know how to find him, but she didn't. Was the soup kitchen even open on weekends? Some weren't.

People didn't stop being hungry on weekends but with the money they saved eating at the soup kitchen during the week often people were able to get by over the weekend. Jake had explained that to her. So, no, she may not be able to find him at the soup kitchen. What about the Salvation Army? But did he work there on weekends? Only one way to find out.

She got out the phone book, looked up the number for the Salvation Army, made an educated guess as to which one Jake worked at, then started calling.

"Hello, is Jake Alexander there?"

"Who, Jake? Just a minute. I'm not sure he comes in today."

"Well, if not could you give me a phone number or address where I can reach him?"

"I'm sorry. We can't give out that information, but just a minute. Let me check his work schedule."

Diane had been relieved to actually hear a human voice. Her first two calls had only reached recordings. At last a human voice and the jackpot. At least she knew where Jake worked. She circled the number in the phone book.

"Hello," the voice returned. "He's not here right now but he should be later this afternoon. Do you want to leave a message?"

"No, that's fine. I'll just call back."

"No one will be here to answer the phone. Jake may not hear it."

"That's okay. I'll take my chances." What was she doing, she asked herself when she hung up. Am I crazy? Crazy or not, she got out a map of the city and located the Salvation Army where Jake worked.

"Now what," she thought. "Do I just show up? Do I wait for him?" Diane wasn't sure what she was going to do. It won't hurt to just drive by the place, she told herself. Besides, it's a nice day. I'll just go for a ride, maybe do some shopping. No big deal. But she knew where she was headed.

Diane drove around the city block where the Salvation Army was several times, coming at it from different directions until she found a parking spot across the street from it. She pulled in then sat and asked herself, "What do I do now? I can't believe I'm here. Do I wait? Do I knock on the door; see if Jake is already here? What? Do I wait for him to leave then follow him home – like a sneak? I'm not a sneak. What am I doing?"

Just then somebody came alongside of her car and rapped on her window.

"Hello stranger, what brings you here?" Jake asked as she rolled down the window.

"Oh, um, I, um," Diane tried to think what to say. Finally she settled on the truth. "I was looking for you."

"Well you found me. I told you you'd be able to find me."

"That you did and I did, find you, I mean." Diane was flustered. She looked back and forth between the steering wheel and Jake's blue eyes. "So how are you?"

"You didn't come all this way just to say that."

"No, I didn't. I didn't know how else to find you. You have to work, don't you?"

"Yes, but I keep my own hours. It doesn't matter when I do it, just so it gets done by a certain time. You want to talk?"

"Yes, yes," Diane was so relieved when he said that. That was what she wanted, wasn't it? Just to talk to him.

"Just a minute. I need to check on some things then I'll be all yours," Jake said. She watched him cross the street and unlock a side door to the building. He was back in a few minutes, carrying a slip of paper in his hand.

"You got some time?" he asked. "I need to check something out."

"Sure. No problem. Get in." He climbed into the passenger side of her car.

"I need to get to this address." He showed her the slip of paper. "I'll direct you. Turn right at the next corner."

They ended up at one of the tenement houses in the area. Jake looked at Diane and around the neighborhood then said, "You better come with me." They walked up the steps of the brick building to the first level.

"Nobody's home," a neighbor called to them.

"Are you sure? I got a message from Esther saying she needed to see me."

"I haven't seen anybody come or go from that apartment for two days."

"That's not like her."

"No, it's not. You want I should call her son?"

"That might be a good idea. I'll try the door." The front door was locked tight. No one answered the doorbell or their knocking. Jake looked for another way into the house. The back door opened upon his touch. "Come on," he said and they walked in.

"Esther, Esther," he called.

"I'm here," a weak voice called back. Jake ran up the stairs to the second floor. He found Esther on the floor in a pool of caked blood.

"What happened?"

"I don't know. I came home from the soup kitchen like usual. I put the cat out the back door, came back up the steps then it all went black. I think I may have hit my head."

"Or been hit. Was anything stolen?" Jake asked.

"Child, I don't know. It was all I could do to get to the phone. I called James but he wasn't home. That's when I left the message for you. I knew you would find me."

"We better call an ambulance and the police."

"No police, Jake, just get me to bed. I'll be fine."

"You need a doctor's care." Jake felt a sticky mass of blood on her head. "You're lucky it stopped bleeding. Looks like someone hit you pretty hard."

"I'm all right, Jake. Don't call the police."

Jake helped her to a chair and looked her straight in the eyes. "Esther, who did this?"

"I don't know, Jake. That's the truth."

"But you have your suspicions, don't you?"

"Yes, but . . ."

"Was it your grandson?" he whispered gently to her.

"That's who I suspect. He was after money for drugs. I wouldn't give him any."

"It's all right. Kaye is trying to reach James. We'll see what he wants to do about this. But you really need medical attention. How long have you been laying there?"

"A day or so. I don't know. He's not a bad boy. It's those drugs. They make him crazy."

"I know. I know. Let me see if I can clean you up a little and get you something to eat. Diane, would you see what's in the kitchen?"

Diane jumped at the sound of her name but obediently searched the kitchen. She came back with hot tea and some crackers she had found. Jake had the caked blood cleaned off. The cut wasn't as deep as they had originally feared.

"Now you eat this, then we'll get you in your bed so you can rest," Jake said.

"I'm not an invalid," Esther insisted.

"Humor me," Jake smiled. He and Diane went into another room. "We'll have to stay with her till her son gets here. I'll see if Kaye was able to reach him."

"But what about the police? Shouldn't they be called?"

"It's a family matter. We'll let Esther and her son take care of it."

"But . . ."

"Stay here with her while I check." Diane went back into the bedroom and sat on the bed next to the chair where Esther sat.

"Do you want anything else? Maybe some soup?"

"That sounds good, child. I am hungry now that I think of it. But I can get it myself." Esther started to stand up then got dizzy and sat back down. "Maybe not."

"You let me take care of it," Diane said patting her hand.

"Jake's a good man," Esther said, grasping her hand back.

"Yes, he is." Diane slipped her hand out of Esther's and went back to the kitchen for some soup. After finishing the soup Diane helped Esther from the chair to the bed. She sat beside her and continued to hold her hand. That was where Jake and James found her.

"Mama, you all right?" James asked.

"I'm fine, son, thanks to these fine people."

"You better rest."

"That I am," Esther said as she shut her eyes.

James escorted Jake and Diane to the door. "Thank you so much for your help. I'll take it from here."

"You know she thinks Tyrone did it," Jake said.

"I'll take care of that, too. This is family business. Thank you for your help."

"Let us know if we can do anything else," Jake said as he and James shook hands.

"That was a lot of excitement, enough for one day," Jake said as they walked down the steps.

"Yes, more than enough. Do you need to get to work?"

"I probably should. Maybe we can talk tomorrow."

"But how do I find you?"

"How about I find you, at the park where we met. One o'clock tomorrow."

"Sure," she said as she dropped him off at the Army. "See you there."

What a day, she thought as she drove back across town to her apartment. A far cry from what she had expected, but then the unexpected seemed to be the norm where Jake was concerned. She unlocked the door to her apartment and was greeted by her hungry cat. She fed the cat and herself then settled down for the night. There was a message on her machine from John but she decided not to answer it just yet. Not yet, she told herself, maybe tomorrow.

Chapter 6

The morning seemed to go on forever. Never before had a morning seemed so long. She was used to her days, especially her mornings, just sliding by as if there were no tomorrow. Usually they were already gone before they had begun. But this morning was different. It seemed one o'clock would never get here. She returned John's phone call and caught him just before leaving for the week.

"I'm sorry, John. It was so late when I got in yesterday. I didn't want to call. Where was I? . . . shopping with friends. My friend Marge had come up for the day. You remember I told you about her . . . You too. Have a good trip. I'll see you when you get back." Diane hung up the phone with relief. Funny how the lies just seem to trip off her tongue these days. When he gets back, I'll have to tell him the truth then. When he gets back, not before that though.

She didn't want to seem too anxious to see Jake again. There was always plenty to do in the apartment even if what she did was sit in the window-seat and watch the world go by. There was so much to do but nothing that was worth doing. She could clean out a closet or organize the junk drawer. The thought occurred to her to go to church, but for some reason something in her resisted this thought. Not today, not this Sunday. God would understand, even if she didn't.

Thoughts of the other day filled her head. What would today bring, she wondered? More of what happened yesterday? She wasn't sure what she thought. He was different from every other man she had known and yet strangely familiar. That both intrigued her and bothered her. Was it the differences or the familiar that attracted her, she wondered as she drank another cup of coffee.

She was ready to leave at twelve. Mustn't let him think I'm too eager, she thought as she tried to come up with odds and ends to fill her time. But then, something told her she could be herself with this man. If only she knew what that was. At twelve twenty she was out the door. It was a twenty-minute drive through traffic to the park. And then there was parking, always a challenge even on a Sunday. She didn't want to be too early but she definitely didn't want to be late. She made it to the park in record time and found a parking spot within reasonable walking distance and was seated on the park bench where they had first met by ten minutes to one. How was that for timing, she told herself as she looked about the park. She decided to kill the few minutes of extra time going through her planner, looking at the week ahead. She tried not to notice when the clock struck one and then again the quarter hour.

"He must have got hung up somewhere. After all he doesn't have a way to contact me," she reassured herself. "I'll give him till one thirty," she thought just as a hand reached out for hers and she looked up into those amazing blue eyes.

"Sorry I'm late," he said and sat down beside her. "Been waiting long?"

"Not too long." Just all of my life a voice inside her said. "Besides it's a beautiful day. What better place to spend it?"

"It's getting more beautiful all the time," Jake said with a smile that made Diane forget everything she had planned all morning to say. All the things she had meant to ask.

"Did you have any plans?" he asked.

"Well, no, not exactly. Did you have something in mind?"

"Come with me," he said and took her hand as they both stood up. Diane wondered what was going to happen next. Not another funeral she hoped or another afternoon like yesterday. "There's a zoo close by. Have you visited it yet?"

"No, actually I haven't. I've been meaning to, just never seemed to get around to it."

"Then it's about time you did. You don't get around to doing much do you?" he said with a smile.

"What do you mean by that?" Diane found herself taken aback by this affront to her work ethic. She did a lot.

"You don't get around to doing much that's fun, those fun little things that make life worthwhile."

"I guess not, but then you seem to be just as guilty as me. Appears to me you're always busy helping people."

"Maybe, that's why I go to the zoo and to the park."

"To find ladies in distress?"

"No, you were a lucky break, a chance in a life-time. I go to enjoy God's outdoors, nature, the animals. I go to get away from people for a while."

The zoo was crowded with people, families with youngsters in tow, babies in strollers, couples holding hands.

"Seems an unlikely place to get away from people," Diane commented as they bumped through the crowded ticket gate and finally were able to get a little space.

Jake laughed. "That's why I come during the week in the off season. Come on." They walked slowly through the crowd to the different exhibits. They watched the rhinoceros grab branches and pick off leaves using his upper lip.

"It's a prehensile lip – whatever that means," Diane read on the sign.

"It works like the opposing thumb on human hands. Helps the rhinoceros eat leaves without the use of hands. Did you ever try to eat a leaf off of a tree with just your lips?"

"Can't say that I have."

"Here, try it. It's not as easy as it looks. Kind of like trying to take a bite out of an apple dangling from a string with your hands tied behind your back. Try it." He nudged a branch towards her with his mouth.

"No, Jake, not here. All these people," she laughed as he continued to try to grab a bite. "Come on, let's get out of here," she pulled him away laughing.

"See, it's not easy," he mumbled around the leaf he had managed to get into his mouth. "Oh, and look at the spider monkeys. They don't have thumbs. They rely on their tails almost like a thumb on a hand," he said as they walked over to the monkey cage.

"Thank God you can't imitate that," Diane said, then thought better of it as Jake began to make monkey faces. "Forget I said that. Is there anything you can't do?"

"I can't read a mind or heal a broken heart, but I sure do try." Diane looked away in embarrassment as he said that.

"Come on, let's go to the bird house. I love to look at the different colors and varieties of birds from all over the world. Sometimes I dream about going to those places, Africa, South America, Asia, Australia. It's so much more colorful and exciting than here, but then I look at our birds, the owl, the eagle, the gold finch, and I know I am home and it's a good place to be. As good as any." They wandered for a while amidst the crowds in the bird house until they had seen their fill. Then they found a place outside to sit.

"You said you wanted to talk," Jake stated as they sat down.

"Yes, I did," Diane searched her mind for all of those well-rehearsed questions she had wanted to ask. They were not coming to the surface like she wanted them to. Finally she said, "I know so little about you. Tell me something about your life, what you did before."

"Not a lot to tell."

"Were you married?"

"Yes."

"Children?"

"Yes, two boys, one girl."

"What happened? Where are they today?"

"Look," Jake pointed to two bear cubs playing together and the small children watching. "This is a good place for watching my favorite animal." The parents with the kids pulled the reluctant children away from the exhibit as the two year old started to cry. "Mostly I come to watch the animals. I see enough of human behavior out there on the street. But sometimes I like to watch people, too. You can really be alone in a crowd. Sometimes it's easier to be alone in a crowd than when there are only a few other people here and you keep running into them over and over. It's a good place to think."

"What do you think about?"

"Life, mostly. My life, some. Other people's lives, some. Sometimes I just thank God for the day and being alive."

"So what about your kids?"

"They're pretty much grown, except for my daughter. She's a senior this year. Her brothers are both in college. They don't want to have anything to do with me. Their mom's made sure of that. Not that I blame her. She blames me, and rightly so. I'm the one who left. I'm the one who gave up, on her, on the marriage, but not my kids. It just seemed I had my priorities all wrong and by the time I finally realized it, it was too late. The kids had been growing up without me. I didn't know how to get back into their lives and they didn't seem to want me anyway. I guess it was easier to just leave. They're happier, at least it seems that way."

"What did you do?"

"Stock trading, investment banking. What didn't I do? I was on the rise in the corporate world. My wife, she loved it, loved the prestige and the money, but me, it just wasn't me. By the time I realized that, Laura was so accustomed to the life we were leading she wasn't willing or just couldn't try anything else. So I tried to hold on. I tried to talk to her, but she couldn't see. So then I thought I had to keep up the façade for her sake and the kids' sake, but I just couldn't. After several years of this, I finally decided I just couldn't do it any longer so I left. I left the only way I knew how. I knew I couldn't count on Laura for any support. I knew she wouldn't understand. So I bailed out, left her everything and disappeared for a while.

"That was three, four, years ago. My only regret is the kids. Laura remarried. She married a business associate of mine, another rising young star on the corporate scene. She was the perfect executive's wife. I just wasn't the perfect executive that she had thought I was. Fun fact: did you know that around ten percent of the people on Wall Street are psychopaths? I heard about this study the other day. Personally I think the numbers are too low. They all thought I was the crazy one. Still think so. Sometimes I think so too. But that's enough about me. You don't need to hear any sad tales. There are plenty enough of them to go around. I see that every day. So what about you?"

"Oh," Diane was taken aback by his redirecting the conversation back to her. "Well, there's Michael, my son whom I already told you about."

"Yes, how's everything with him?"

"Okay, so far, as far as I know. He hasn't emailed or called but my 'spies' don't have anything too bad to report. No news . . ."

"Yeah, is good news sometimes."

"Sometimes. And then there's Adrian. She's in college and very upset with her wayward mother for trying to have a life of her own."

"What about your former husband?"

"He left us over twelve years ago. I don't hear from him which is fine with me, although I worry about the kids. He was an alcoholic. I don't know where he is now. He never sent any child support and I never asked for any. I guess I just wanted my life back. I didn't want to be beholden to anyone, especially not this man. Maybe that was wrong but . . . Somehow I managed alone. I brought the kids up, paid my own way."

"Sounds like you have much to be proud of."

"Think so? I don't think so. Sometimes I feel like I'm drowning, like I can barely keep my head above water. You know, it still hurts."

"The divorce?"

"Yes, no," Diane's voice cracked a little. "No. No, I don't know what it is that hurts. It hurts that my life, my life just didn't turn out like I had always hoped and dreamed. Never in my wildest dreams did I think I would end up raising two kids alone. I'm not sure what I had thought, but that wasn't part of it."

"You dreamed of love forever, till death do us part?"

"Yes, I thought love was forever. Foolish dream, life has proved that."

"Life has a way of doing that, but I've found that reality is always better than a dream. It has substance and shape. A dream is flimsy. It can blow away unless it becomes rooted in reality. The life I was living, it was a dream. It was some people's dream, but it wasn't mine. It wasn't real. It became a nightmare. So I gave it all up for a dose of reality, and you know what, I'd never go back. Not ever. I'd take today's reality over yesterday's dreams any time."

"I don't want to go back either. My life may not have been a dream but it's mine, what I've made of it. But still . . . I wish I had a dream, a dream that I was meant to fulfill. I think I've stopped dreaming and I don't know how to start again." Diane surprised herself even as she said it. "Sometimes my life seems so empty, especially with the kids gone. I don't want that life back, but I also don't know what I want. Once I knew what I wanted. Now I don't know what I want. I wish I knew."

Jake sat in silence with her then squeezed her hand and said, "Give it time. It'll come. You'll know when it's time."

"I guess so," Diane stated reluctantly.

"I know so," Jake stated with conviction. "Come on, the best is yet to come. You haven't seen my favorite exhibit. Let's see if the polar bears are putting on a show for everyone today." They walked past the two lions sunning themselves peacefully on a large rock and the pacing Siberian tiger to join the crowd around the polar bear exhibit. Going down below the water tank they were able to watch the underwater antics of one of the large bears as it playfully swam by.

"They seem to take so much pleasure in swimming and playing. That's what they were made to do. When you find what you were made to do, you'll be like that too. It'll be like second nature."

"Will it?" Diane asked with a smile. "And have you found what you were made for?"

"Maybe," Jake gazed seriously into her eyes. "Maybe I have. It feels good, worthwhile, like I'm making a difference no matter how small. My life has meaning."

They snacked on popcorn and ice cream while wandering through the rest of the exhibit. They laughed at the antics of children and animals, chuckling as one toddler tried to catch one of the many peacocks strolling through the zoo. Reluctantly they decided to call it a day.

"I've got to work tomorrow, and I suppose you've got to work tonight."

"Yes, I do." Jake walked her back to her car.

"Thank you so much for today. It's been so long since I've been to the zoo. Tom and I used to go, and I used to take Adrian and Michael when they were little. That was such a long time ago. It brought back so many memories."

"Hopefully we've made a few new ones, too."

"Yes, we have. Thank you for giving me a reason to come to the zoo again. Can I give you a lift anywhere?" Diane asked as she put her hand on the car door handle.

"No, that's all right."

"Are you sure? It's no bother. Which reminds me, how do I get a hold of you if I want to? And don't give me that line about knowing how to find you."

"It's worked, hasn't it?"

"By chance, yes. I don't want to leave it to chance that we'll meet again, do you?" Diane turned and looked him deep in the eyes.

"No, it won't be by chance. We'll meet again," Jake stated seriously. "You can reach me at the Salvation Army. I check my messages every day."

"Don't you want my phone number? Don't you want my address?"

"I know how to find you," he said, smiling once again. "Remember, I know where you work."

Diane began to feel flustered. "Look. Even if you won't give me your address and phone number, I want you to have mine." She slipped him a piece of paper. "Call me, okay, call me," she said as she climbed into her car. She felt like she was almost pleading with him. He'll never call; she heard a voice say in her head.

Just where is this relationship going, Diane thought with some frustration as she drove home. Such a wonderful day. Such a good time. But why wouldn't he give her his phone number? Why wouldn't he tell her where he lives? Why does it always have to be up to her to contact him? A little too one-sided, she thought. She didn't like that.

"Maybe he doesn't have a phone. Have you thought about that?" the voice of her friend sounded in her head.

"Everybody's got a phone," she responded.

"Street people don't have phones or apartments. Maybe that's why."

"Maybe. I don't know. I just want him to call me for a change. Ask me out. Like a real relationship and a real date." Was this real or just made up in her head? The dialogue went on in her head till she got home. Don't let it ruin a beautiful day she told herself as she walked into her apartment.

She noticed that the light in the spare bedroom was on. She didn't remember turning it on. Samantha didn't appear begging for her dinner. What was going on? She heard the sound of someone moving in one of the bedrooms. She was ready to run out the door and call the police from her cell phone, only to see Michael walk out into the living room, rubbing his wet head with a towel.

"Michael?!" she said with a start.

"That's right. Where have you been?"

"Out. What are you doing here?"

"I thought I still lived here. You told me I could come back any time I wanted. I still had my key, so here I am."

"I know I said that, but I guess I thought I would get more notice than this."

"Hey, look, if you don't want me here, I'm out of here."

"No, no. Don't go. I was just taken aback because I didn't expect you. What happened?"

"Nothing. Nothing ever happens in that dead town. That's why I left." More likely he had a run in with his friends and got kicked out for not paying his share of the rent, but Diane wasn't going to bring that up. Marge might be able to find out for her. She was just happy he was home, or was she?

"So who's this John guy?" Michael asked as he placed the towel over a kitchen chair.

"John?"

"Yeah, he called while you were out."

"Oh, just a friend."

"Sounded like he thought he was more than that."

"How much did he say to you?"

"Enough," Michael smiled and plopped down on the couch. Diane realized he was just teasing.

"The old rules still apply," she reminded him.

"Yeah, yeah, I know. You don't have to remind me. Anything to eat?"

"Help yourself to anything in the refrigerator."

"Already have," he said with a grin. That was her old Michael. Diane smiled back.

"It's good to see you again."

"You too, Mom." She prepared them both a snack then excused herself and went to bed. It had been a long day.

Chapter 7

With Michael home she didn't have a lot of time to worry about Jake. Michael had agreed to go back to school that fall and was even talking about getting a job so he could pay her parents back the money they had loaned him. She didn't know what all had happened that summer. She didn't ask and Michael didn't volunteer any information. Whatever had happened, he seemed a little more willing to cooperate with her. All that she was able to find out from Marge was that there had been some kind of misunderstanding. Drugs may have been involved.

She worried about him being alone in the apartment while she was at work. She worried about him job hunting. She didn't know what was worse, having him lay around the apartment all day or having him out looking for work and finding who knows what kind of trouble. She was relieved when school started. At least then she knew where he was all day and something of what he was doing. Then he managed to get a job after school at a gas station and convenience store.

"It doesn't pay a lot, but it's a start. Maybe I'll be able to buy a car soon," Michael told her. She was impressed with this new found work ethic. She just hoped it lasted for more than a week. He seemed to be okay about school too, not enthusiastic but okay. That was all she could ask.

"I don't want to be working at a gas station all my life, right. So I guess I'll graduate," he told her. Something must have happened over the summer. Perhaps just a dose of reality. Perhaps that was all he had needed to get him back on track. She hoped so.

Michael was certainly more than enough reason to get her mind off of Jake. And then there was John, who continued to be attentive. He had called her the night after Michael moved back.

"I hear Michael's back. How is it going?"

"So far, so good. He seems to have matured a little over the summer."

"A few months on your own can do that to someone. He sounded like a pretty good kid on the phone."

Yes, he is, he is a pretty good kid, Diane thought afterwards. She kept reminding herself of that. John had met Michael. They were cordial to each other; somewhat sizing each other up, but cordial. John realized their relationship was still too tentative to withstand a frontal assault by a teenage son. Michael was unsure about this man in his mother's life. There had been so many changes. He wasn't ready for another one, yet he realized his mother needed a life of her own, just like he did. That was beginning to sink in. He didn't want her living her life for him, but it was hard to give up the privilege of being the only man in her life. If only he had known his father, he thought with regret.

He wasn't sure why that thought was coming back to him now. Once, when he was eight, he had tried to run away from home. He had been going to find his dad. That was what he had told his mom when she found him at the bus station. His mom had fought back the tears as she explained that he was nowhere to be found.

"I don't believe you," he had said. "I'll find him."

"How will you do that?"

"I'm going to grandma and grandpa's. They will help me."

"I wish they could. They don't know where he is either. I'm sorry, Michael. Your dad does not want to be found. You just have to accept that. And you know what, it's his loss because he's missing out on knowing two great kids," she had said as she hugged him. She took him out for ice cream before going back home.

"Look, Dad's a jerk," Adrian had told him that night. "He's not coming back. You better accept it."

"He is not a jerk," he had yelled at Adrian and they began to fight. They had not told their mother what the fight had been about, but he knew she suspected it. That was the last he had ever said anything about his dad, but he still thought about him from time to time. He liked to imagine what he was like. He had been so young when his dad had left. Not quite five. He liked to imagine that his dad was proud of him, that he was still looking out for him from a distance. Michael just couldn't see him. He wondered if his dad ever thought about him. He had tried to talk to Adrian about it.

"Do you ever wonder about Dad? Where he is? What he's doing?"

"No, and you shouldn't either." Adrian had been older when their dad had left. She had been nine. She remembered so much more than he did. She remembered their dad being gone for days at a time. How their mother had worried. And then nights coming home drunk. Mom had tried to hide it from them, but Adrian had seen. She knew. She knew how there was never enough money for the extras her friends had like new clothes, bikes, money to go to the movies. That had changed when their dad had moved out. Their mom had started to work full-time, money was still tight but at least it was there. It could be counted on. And now and then there was money for nice things, little extras she hadn't had before. She had had to do more around the house to help her mom out, but then that really was no different. She no longer had to worry about her dad coming home drunk. She no longer had to worry about that worried look on her mother's face nights her dad didn't come home. Life had been better once it was just their mom and them.

But Michael didn't see that. He hadn't known their dad. Those memories he did have, he colored in his mind. He denied the fact that he had smelled alcohol on his dad's breath when he had kissed him goodnight. He remembered his dad being gone, but that had been business. He had been on important business trips and that was what had kept him away from home. And then one day he went on a business trip and didn't come back. His mother had tried to explain that his dad had gone away.

"He'll come back, though. He always comes back," Michael had said.

"Not this time. He won't be coming back."

"Did he die?"

"No."

"Then he'll come back. I know he will. What did you do to him? Why did you send him away?" he had angrily accused her of driving his father away. In his loss and anger he had blamed his mom at first. But then grandpa had stepped in, his dad's dad. He had tried to explain it to Michael. Michael had not understood, but he tried not to blame his mother.

"Your dad's got big ideas, big dreams. He's left to follow those dreams," grandpa had said.

"Then he'll come back some day. He'll come back for me."

"I don't think there's room for you in those dreams right now."

"Not now, but later. He'll come back for me later."

"I don't know, son. I don't think so." He had not wanted to speak against his own son, but he knew Tom wasn't coming back, knew it in his heart. How could he tell this to his grandson and rob him of all hope?

Tom had been a salesman. Often he was on the road. Often he didn't come home. Diane had been getting used to it. Then one day, he told her about another job opportunity, another dream to follow. He was going first. He'd send for her and the kids once he was settled. That's what he had told her. She knew it wasn't the truth. She knew, maybe there was a job, but once gone he would not look back. He had wanted out of this town for some time now. He had blamed her often enough for keeping him here.

"You and these kids. You've got me trapped in this crummy town in this crummy job. I could do so much better if it wasn't for you," he used to say in a drunken rage.

She knew he wasn't coming back to get them. He had said he would be better off without her and the kids, so she decided to give him what he had wanted. He had called a few times at first. Then the calls had stopped, just as she had expected. Each time he had asked how the kids were and had assured her his big break was coming. He'd say he would send for her and the kids soon. He didn't give her his address. She had no way to get in touch with him.

"As soon as I get settled, I'll give you my address," he had assured her. She knew it would not be happening.

It had taken some time, but she managed to get a divorce. She had been hesitant to do it at first because it just hadn't seemed like the right thing to do. Christian women don't divorce, she had told herself, even when the minister had urged her to go ahead.

"You need to go on with your life. Your kids need a father." Finally she had decided to file for a divorce. Her lawyer had tried unsuccessfully to track Tom down.

"I told you, if Tom didn't want to be found, he would not be found," she had told him. Finally they filed the papers without him. It was seven years before she was free, but she didn't feel free.

Michael missed his dad, but he knew enough not to talk to his mom about him. Whenever he mentioned him that tight expression appeared on her face. She had been unhappy for so long. He didn't want to add to it. He had worried about her, too. As hard as this past year had been, he could see his mom was, well, almost happy. She seemed to like the changes. And now there was this man in her life, calling her up, taking her out. Michael resented him. After all, he wasn't his dad. He was surprised by his resentment.

"So who's this Jake character?" Michael asked. Diane's heart leaped into her throat at the mention of his name.

"Who?"

"Jake Alexander. He left a message for you on the answering machine."

"Oh, just a friend I made over the summer," Diane tried to sound nonchalant. She thought she had managed to forget about him. She had been so busy with Michael and work, and then there was John as well.

"Just a friend," she repeated. She fought to keep her hand from shaking as she pushed the button of her answering machine.

"Hi, Diane. It's Jake Alexander. It's good to hear your voice. I was hoping to talk to you, but I guess not. I'll try another time." It was good to hear his voice, too. He didn't sound quite so self-assured on the answering machine. He almost seemed uncertain about calling. Her heart was racing as she listened to the message. No return phone number. Now what was she to do? Wait for him to call back? Maybe. She wasn't sure.

"And how's John?" Michael's voice was tinged with sarcasm.

"He's fine, just fine," she answered. They had been out to eat again. "You hungry?"

"Isn't that the third time this week you had dinner with him?"

"Why, I guess so, if you are counting. I wasn't counting. By the way, I invited him over for dinner tomorrow."

"Thanks for the warning. I'll make sure I'm not here."

"But Michael, I was hoping . . ." Michael stormed off to his bedroom before she could finish. She had been hoping they could eat together. She wanted Michael to have a chance to get to know John better. At first Michael had seemed receptive to John being in her life, but now she didn't know what was going on.

And why did Jake have to call now? How she had wanted him to call after their last Sunday together. She had hoped he would call and yet was almost relieved when he didn't. Obviously this relationship had no future – was going nowhere. You couldn't build a relationship on chance encounters in the park. John was so much more reliable and dependable. He was everything she wanted in a relationship. Couldn't Michael see that? Couldn't she see that, she tried to convince herself.

And now, after a month of no calls, Jake has to come back into her life. What was she to do now? She guessed she had to see him, or talk to him, at least one more time, to say goodbye. But who was she fooling? They hadn't even kissed. He was just a friend, a casual acquaintance. It wouldn't hurt to see him again, and to keep on seeing him, as a friend, right? They were just friends. Then why did her heart beat so at the mention of his name?

She jumped as the phone rang. Someone for Michael. She didn't recognize the voice, but at least Michael appeared to be making friends. She called to him then retired to her room and her own thoughts for the night.

The thought of Jake's phone call stayed with her all the next morning. If she could have done it without raising suspicions in Michael, she would have saved the message in order to play it over and over again. Instead all she had was the memory of his voice going over and over in her brain.

She decided she needed some fresh air and went for a walk on her lunch break. She thought about going to the park or maybe to the zoo on the offhand chance she might run into Jake. How obvious, she told herself. Instead she made her way into a church downtown. The side door had been left open for anyone who needed a quiet space to pray. That was what she really needed, she thought.

She walked into the dimly lit church. Bits of sunlight lit up isolated spots, adding color to the darkness through stained glass windows. A few other individuals had sought out the quiet of the building. She slipped into a pew several rows up from the entrance and tried to pray.

What do I do now, dear God? I'm so confused. Why does this man haunt my memories and my dreams? I've known him for such a short time. Yet he touches something in me from long ago. Stay away, part of me says. Come closer, another says. I don't know where it's all coming from or where it's going. And then there's Michael and his resistance to John being in my life. Maybe I should just forget about dating for a while, until Michael gets more settled. Hasn't he been through enough this past year? Maybe I'm moving too fast. What do you think, God? What would you have me do?

No answer, not that she expected one. Why should now be any different from other times? Still she sensed God's presence was here. Why didn't he answer? Then she sensed another presence, slipping into the pew behind her.

"Diane?" Diane jumped as she heard the familiar voice. Dared she turn around?

"Jake?" she said to the figure who had come up behind her, leaning forward in the pew.

"None other," he smiled as she turned and looked into his baby blue eyes. "I didn't expect to find you here."

"Nor I, you!" she stated emphatically then blushed as the other visitors turned to stare at her.

"Let's get out of here," Jake said. Diane rose in agreement. She shivered as he put his arm around her and escorted her to the door. "Cold?" he asked.

"Just a little," she lied. But it wasn't a complete lie. It seems she had gone both hot and cold at the sight of him and his touch.

"Let's get into the sun. It is getting a bit nippy, isn't it?" They walked until they found a bench that was in the sun. "Want some coffee or hot chocolate?"

"No, I'm fine. Just fine," Diane pulled her coat about her.

"It's good to see you. Did you get my message?" Jake asked.

"Yes, but I had no way to return it."

"I was going to call again," they both spoke so fast one barely finished before the other started in. They laughed and smiled at each other.

"Where have you been?" Jake asked.

"I might ask you the same thing," Diane responded.

"I've been where I've always been. The usual routine."

"Your routine is far from routine," Diane laughed.

"You knew how to reach me if you wanted to."

"Yes, I did. I just wanted to know if you wanted me to . . . Oh, never mind. Michael's back."

"That's great!"

"Yeah, I think so too. So far it's been working out pretty good. He's back in school. He's even got at a part-time job at a gas station."

"Which one?"

"The Stop and Go on the corner of West and Elm."

"You mean the Stop and Rob."

"Please don't remind me."

"That's great. I'll check it out sometime. When does he work?"

"After school. Some nights, but not late. I don't want him working too late. It's too dangerous."

"Good thinking. You'll have to introduce me. I'll put out a good word for him on the street."

"Would you do that? I'd really appreciate it. I do worry."

"Don't worry. That's not too bad a part of town. He should be fine as long as he keeps his wits about him. And what about you? Any new promotions yet?"

"No, no. I have to be here for a year first. I'll be around for a while."

"Good, I'm glad to hear it. How about you play hooky, just for today? Have some fun?" She recognized that look and the lure of attraction in his voice. Just like Tom when they had started dating as teenagers. "What's one day? They'll hardly know you're gone." Tom had talked her into skipping that one beautiful spring day. They had spent it together, gone for a picnic in the park, a walk along the river bank and he had proposed. She had been so young. Just a senior in high school, Michael's age. He had been older, so much more mature. How could she have said no back then?

"No," she shook her head firmly. "No, I can't."

"Then how about tonight? Can I see you tonight?"

"No, I don't know." Dinner with Michael and John. That's right. She had plans she reminded herself. "I've got plans."

"I'm sorry. I should have known. You're busy. You can't just drop things in a moment's notice," there was a sad recognition in his voice, like he had done this before.

"No, I can't just drop things on a moment's notice. I've got responsibilities, people who depend on me. Plans. I need some advance notice. I can't just jump because someone calls." She found herself getting angry.

"Hey, that's all right. Maybe some other time."

"There won't be another time, will there, Jake?" Diane asked.

"What do you mean, there won't be another time? Of course there will be."

"No, there won't because you can't plan more than one day in advance. You want everything to be free and easy, respond to the moment, carpe diem. Well, I can't live that way. I have responsibilities, commitments. I need someone I can rely on to be there when he says he will be."

"Hey, when was I not there for you?" Jake asked. Diane turned aside with her back to him. "Look, is this about me or somebody else? I don't know who it was who hurt you and left you so distrusting, but it wasn't me. You hardly know me. Was it Michael's dad?"

Diane refused to answer him.

"Look. I don't know what's going on here, but I can't help if you don't talk to me. What do I have to do?"

"Just leave me alone," Diane said. "I have to get to work." Diane got up abruptly and walked away from there. She didn't know why she felt like crying. The tears hung at the corner of her eyes, where she willed them to go away. She couldn't go back to work like this. She knew that much. She fumbled for a tissue in her purse when a large hand handed her a handkerchief. She accepted it without looking up, knowing full well who it belonged to.

"I always keep a fresh supply available for women in distress." Diane tried to laugh at Jake's feeble joke.

"I'm sorry. I don't know why I said that." She handed back his handkerchief.

"So why don't we talk about it over lunch?"

"I guess I better call the store and let them know I'll be late."

"Here, it's on me." Jake handed her change to use in the pay phone on the corner. She laughed and pulled out her work cell phone. "No, it's on me," she said, "not everyone can live without an electronic tether like you."

They walked to the park. Jake bought them bratwurst and sauerkraut from a vendor. They sat on a bench by the pond and ate in silence.

"Thank you," Diane said. "Next time lunch will be on me."

"So, there will be a next time," Jake stated with a smile.

"Oh, Jake, I don't know. I don't know why I said what I did or why I got so upset." Jake sat quietly as she composed her thought. "You do remind me of someone. Michael's father, Tom."

"He must have hurt you pretty bad."

"In some ways, but no, as I look back at it now, there were good days. Really wonderful days. He was so charming and full of himself, full of dreams. And I believed him. I bought into his dreams hook, line and sinker. I made them my own. I believed in him. But then he started drinking so much and he would be gone for days at a time. I worried so about him but I didn't know . . . there was nothing I could do. At least nothing I could think of. I just struggled to keep our heads above water, to pay the bills and take care of the kids. We didn't know better, either of us. We were just kids in love, but I was replaced one day by drinking," Diane sighed.

"He went away one day," Diane continued. "Said he had a great business opportunity, and he never came back. I knew he would never come back, knew it in my heart but didn't want to believe it. Nothing. No contact with me. No contact with the kids. There were a few phone calls at first but then, nothing. He didn't want to be found . . . kind of like you."

Jake sat in silence on the bench, staring at the ground.

"Is that what you think? That I'm just like Tom?"

"I don't know. I don't know you too well, but yes, you remind me of Tom. When I'm with you, I feel like I used to feel with Tom. And I'm so afraid."

Jake continued to stare down at the ground. "I don't know what to say, Diane. I'm not Tom, but maybe I could have been. I haven't had contact with my kids for years."

"But at least you tried," Diane interrupted.

"Yeah, but how hard did I try? It was easier to walk away than to try. I won't blame you if you walk away from me. I can't say I'm better than Tom. I don't know the man. I hope I've learned from my mistakes, but there's probably many more mistakes waiting to happen. I just know I enjoy being with you. I love the look of the sunlight on your face, the wind blowing your hair. I like being with you for now. I can't promise you tomorrow. My tomorrows aren't my own. They've been promised to God. I don't know where I'll be a month from now, a week from now, even a day from now, but for now, for today, we're together. I like being with you. I think about you more than I should, more than I have a right to. For now, I think God has brought you into my life, and I have been brought into your life for some reason that is God's. That's enough for me. Is it enough for you?"

"I don't know. I just don't know." Diane paused. "I need time. I've got to think." She glanced at her watch. "I better get back to work. Thank you for the use of your handkerchief." Despite herself she found herself adding as if by habit. "Will I see you again?"

"It's up to you," he said. He stood up and watched as she walked away.

Chapter 8

Diane didn't know how she managed to get through dinner that night, but she did. John tried to talk to Michael who sat in silence then asked to be excused to do his homework. Diane heard music blasting out of his bedroom shortly after he left.

She smiled wanly at John. "Kids," she said.

"It's all right. Remember, I have kids of my own. I remember what those teen years were like. It must be very hard for him right now. Here, let me help with the dishes. By the way, dinner was great." What a charmer, Diane thought. What a gentleman. Far better than . . . but she wasn't going to allow herself to even think his name. At least not now. She couldn't take the chance. John helped her get the dishes rinsed and into the dishwasher. She was about to thank him and say goodnight when he said, "By the way. I've been meaning to tell you but I didn't want to say anything with Michael around."

"Tell me what?" she asked, afraid of what she would hear.

"There's talk of you not having to wait a full year to get a store of your own to manage."

"What, how can that be? I'm not ready."

"I've got a few strings I can pull here and there. And you've been receiving very commendable reports from your supervisor." John smiled at this, thinking Diane would be grateful.

"Thank you, but I'm not ready."

"What do you mean you're not ready? Have some faith in yourself. I do. Besides, I may be transferred soon to another district. You could transfer with me. It could be arranged."

"But John, what about Michael? He's just got back into school. I can't move him again just yet. And I like it here. I'm not sure I want to leave. Three moves in one year is a bit much. I'd like to finish one year here."

"Look, I don't want to pressure you. Besides there's nothing definite yet. Just think about it."

"I will, now if you'll excuse me, I think I'd like to get ready for bed."

"I'm sorry, dear. Maybe I shouldn't have said anything yet. I thought you'd be happy."

"It's all right. I am, kind of, I guess. Maybe I just need to sleep on it." She said good-bye just as the phone rang. She didn't recognize the number on Caller ID. Michael certainly couldn't hear it. She decided not to answer it but let her machine take the call.

"Hi, Diane, it's Jake. I'm sorry about this afternoon. I just wanted to check and see if you were all right. Anyway, maybe we can talk sometime."

She fought the urge to pick up the phone before he hung up, then scrambled to write down the number. Where had he been calling from? A pay phone? The Army? The soup kitchen? Part of her wanted to go out into the night and find him. But she couldn't. Too much, her brain kept saying. Too much. You need time to think, she told herself. Things might look different in the morning.

They didn't look too different the next morning. Michael hurried off to school with hardly a grunt in her direction. She fingered the phone number she had written down last night but decided she better wait. Fortunately John was going to be out of town for a few days at another store so she didn't have to deal with him. He left a beautiful autumn bouquet of flowers on her desk with a note of thanks for dinner.

Diane fingered the card just as she had fingered the telephone number earlier. What was she to do? She should tell John about Jake, but there is no Jake. He's just a figment of her imagination. He was here today, gone tomorrow. She couldn't count on him. This was real, she thought as she held the card and looked at the flowers. Maybe she should think about a promotion. But what if, what if what Jake had said was right? What if God had brought them together for this moment of time? Why had God brought him into her life? Was she not listening to God? Maybe she did need to see him again, just so she could know.

"So who is this Jake character?" Michael asked as soon as she walked in the door.

"What? Who?" Diane felt her heart flutter at the mention of his name.

"Jake. He keeps calling. There's a message for you on the machine. Is he yet another secret I'm not supposed to know about?"

"There's nothing to know," Diane said faintly as she walked over to her answering machine.

"Hmmm," Michael grumbled in disbelief. "I'm out of here. Got to go to work," he said as he walked out the door.

Ordinarily Diane would have called Michael back and tried to talk to him. Ordinarily. But nothing was ordinary any more, or so it seemed. What was ordinary, normal? There was a time when she thought she knew. Now she had no idea what normal was or whether her life would ever be normal. John was normal, she thought to herself. Hang on to John. He was normal. Jake was . . . something else. She didn't know what. Hesitantly she played the message.

"Hi, Diane, it's Jake. Just wanted to talk to you. Guess you're not home. I'll try again some other time. Bye." Will he? Will he try to call again? Diane hoped so and feared it as well. How long could she, should she, keep up this game of cat and mouse? Who was the cat and who the mouse? Now that he was actually calling her, she didn't know that she felt any better than before when he didn't call. What was she to do next? She didn't have much time to think about it before the phone rang again. Her fingers rested over the receiver, hesitating, wondering, should she pick it up? Was it him? She let the machine take the call. She listened to the familiar voice.

"Hi, Diane, Jake again. I was hoping to catch you home. Your son had said you'd be home by now. Guess he was wrong, or maybe I was wrong to call . . ." There was a pause on the line. "Guess I better go," he started to say as Diane picked up the phone.

"Jake, Jake, is that you? I just got in the door. Hang on while I turn off this stupid machine." Diane fumbled for the on/off switch. "Okay, I'm here."

"Hi. I've been trying to reach you."

"I know. You talked to my son?"

"Yeah. A while ago. Seems like a nice enough kid. Did he give you the message?"

"Well, no, yes and no. He said you had called, but not that he had talked to you. Doesn't matter. How are you?"

"I'm fine. I just wanted to talk, see how you are."

"I'm fine, I guess. Well, actually I'm not all that fine." Diane was embarrassed to hear her voice crack over the phone. "I mean, I'm all right, just . . . can we talk?"

"Sure. When?"

"Now?" They arranged to meet in an hour at an Italian restaurant within walking distance of Diane's apartment. No one knew either of them there and they could sit in a booth with relative privacy.

"You hungry?" Diane asked Jake as he sat down. "My treat, after all you've been treating me all along." Diane hastened to add knowing that chances were that Jake didn't have much money.

"I guess I could eat a little pasta," Jake smiled. He seemed comfortable in the surroundings even in his jeans and work shirt. He'd be comfortable anywhere he went, Diane thought to herself. It wasn't too upscale but more of a mid-scale restaurant with grease spots on the plastic table clothes hidden by the dim lights and candles. It was a good place to be.

Diane ordered Chianti for both of them and an antipasto salad for herself. Jake ordered spaghetti with meatballs.

"So," Jake said once their order was placed. "How are you? Really. You sounded a little confused over the phone."

"Confused, me, no, or yes," Diane stammered. She had been confused on the phone, but now that he was here, sitting across from her, there was nothing to be confused about. All those things that she worried about, thought about when they weren't together seemed unimportant now. They were just a figment of her overactive imagination, she told herself. Or, if not, it wasn't really important anyway.

"What about?" Jake asked and looked at her with those baby blue eyes.

"Oh, nothing. It's not really important. Well, there is a possibility I might be offered a promotion, new store, new city, but it's nothing definite yet. Nothing to worry about." Should she say anything about John, she wondered. But John wasn't who she was confused about. She was confused about him, how she felt about him. But that no longer seemed important.

"You sure?" Jake asked.

"I'm sure." She was sure at that instant. She had never felt so sure. She was sure about one thing. She was happy to be here with this man and that was enough for one night. Let tomorrow take care of tomorrow.

"Was there something in particular you wanted to talk to me about?" she asked him.

"It no longer seems important," he said, and with that they entered into a quiet agreement not to bring up anything that might spoil the evening. They enjoyed the night, the wine, the food, the conversation. Diane didn't want it to end, but by ten-thirty she realized she better be getting home.

"What are you doing this Saturday?" Diane asked before they left to go their separate ways.

"Spending it with you?" Jake asked with a smile.

"Precisely!" Diane laughed. "Let me make the arrangements this time. I'll plan the day. Fair enough?"

"Fair enough," Jake agreed.

"Where should I pick you up?" she asked.

"How about in front of the Army?"

"Ten o'clock?"

"Ten o'clock." They parted with just a squeeze of their hands and a smile. Nothing to indicate that they were more than friends. They were more like two school chums planning on playing hooky to go to the swimming hole. Diane resisted any attempt to try and find out where Jake lived. It was enough just to be together. They were just friends out to have a good time together. No reason for feeling any guilt about that. They were going to keep it safe, keep this relationship safe, Diane reassured herself as she walked into her apartment building. The relationship felt good and safe and fun. She liked that. She had decided that she liked that and wanted to keep it that way.

Michael was home from his shift at work when she got home.

"Have you been drinking?" he asked her suspiciously as she walked in the door.

"Just a little drink with a good friend."

"Smells like more than a little to me," he said waiting to pick a fight. "Oh, by the way, John called while you were out. The message is on the machine."

"John, oh, thank you, Michael. I'll call him in the morning." A glimmer of guilt tried to break through but she fought it off with a yawn. "I'm going to bed." She was in far too good a mood to allow herself to come down just yet.

The mood continued for the rest of the week as she looked forward to Saturday. Her employees commented on how happy she seemed to be, attributing it to her relationship with John. Michael, when he was around, just grunted and ignored her. For once Diane didn't let it bother her. She was preoccupied with plans for Saturday. This time she was going to be the one calling the shots, she told herself.

She arrived at the Army precisely at ten o'clock. Jake was late as she was beginning to realize was his custom. She thought about going inside and asking for him, just as he showed up and climbed in the passenger seat of the car. She was determined to let nothing ruin this day.

"Where to?" Jake asked with a smile.

"You'll see when we get there." He looked so trim and handsome in his jeans and army jacket. Diane smiled internally but didn't want him to know how happy she was to see him. "It's good you wore a jacket," she commented.

"Aha, a clue. We're going to be outdoors."

"That's all the clues you'll get out of me," Diane responded. They chatted casually as Diane drove out of the city. She asked about different people she had met at the soup kitchen. He asked about Michael and Adrian and her job.

Finally they reached the outskirts of the city. Diane pulled down a dirt road. "I hope this is the right road," she said, then saw the sign for the apple orchard she was looking for. Next to the orchard was a small store and deli with homemade baked goods and sandwiches. "One of my employees told me about this place. She said they had great picnic lunches." They both got out of her car, walked around the grounds of the orchard, then headed into the store. After looking at the variety of foods available, together they picked out what they wanted for lunch. Their hands fit naturally together as they walked about the store. Diane didn't resist this gesture of friendship; she felt reassured by the warmth and strength of his grip. The store owner placed the items they chose in a picnic basket and filled the thermos Diane had brought with hot cider.

"It's a bit nippy out there, especially in the shade," he said as he rang up the items on the cash register.

"How far is it from here to the nature reserve?" Diane asked as she paid the bill.

"Not too far. Just about five miles down the road. There's a sign on the right. You can't miss it."

"Thanks," Diane said. Jake picked up the basket and loaded it in the back seat of the car.

"Nature reserve?" he commented as they got back in.

"Yes, you forget. I'm a small town girl. You've shown me the city. I'll show you the country."

Jake smiled in response and reached over and briefly took her hand from the steering wheel. "Wherever you go, I'll go."

"You don't have a choice," Diane said with a smile as she put her hand back on the steering wheel.

"Oh, I have a choice. There's always a choice," Jake said. They drove the rest of the way in silence.

Diane turned at the sign for the nature center. It was not as secluded as she had thought.

"Looks like lots of other people had the same idea," Diane said as they pulled into the crowded parking lot.

"Lots of city folk trying to enjoy a little country," Jake agreed. "We'll find our space."

And that they did once they got on to the trails. The trees were ablaze with autumn colors.

"It's just as I hoped," Diane commented as they walked amid the trees. "I miss the trees so much living in the city. Sure there are trees, but it's just not the same." They climbed up to one of the highest points and looked out on the view of a small pond and marsh area amidst the trees. "This is precisely what I've been missing, what I needed," Diane said as Jake squeezed her hand. They shared the view with the other city folk, all hungry for a bit of country.

"Let's find a good place to eat," Diane said as the viewing area got a little too crowded for her comfort. The picnic tables were already occupied so they proceeded to walk further along the trail looking for a place not too crowded with people or mosquitoes that inhabited the lower areas of the marsh lands. They were almost ready to give up on picnicking when they found a meadow area somewhat off the beaten path. They weren't sure whether it was part of the nature area or belonged to a neighboring farmer, but decided to take their chances. They spread out a doubled over blanket and sat down to eat. The ground was a little chilly and of course there were the inevitable bugs that had to invade their space.

"Don't worry, they won't eat too much," Jake reassured her as they brushed away uninvited guests.

"Maybe this wasn't such a great idea after all," Diane said as a leaf landed into her cider cup.

"Hey, it's just fine. So tell me, why did you lure this committed city boy out to the bug-infested country? To what purpose?" Jake said with a grin.

"No purpose. No reason. I just thought it would be fun, a nice change of pace. I've always loved the fall, the changing weather, changing trees, changing me . . . Fall's a time of letting go."

"And just what are you letting go of?"

"I don't know. I'm not sure just what, just yet. I just know I am. Aren't we all, aren't we always letting go of parts of our life at different times? Sometimes, as I watch the leaves of a tree be stripped off till the tree is bare, I feel that that's me being stripped. I ask God, what is it I have to let go of today? I trust that God will take care of the rest as long as I'm open to whatever God wants for me."

She paused and wrapped her fingers around her cup of cider. "You know, you said you thought it was God who brought us together … why?"

"Why? I don't know. I think it was more than chance that the two of us should meet like we did. That we ran into each again at the church. There's a reason why we did. There's a reason why I think about you so much. There's a reason, but I don't know what it is."

Diane turned her head aside as he said that. She was scared. She had both wanted to hear that, and didn't want to. She was afraid of where it might lead her.

"I think about you too, too much," she said while looking down. "I shouldn't."

"Why not?"

"There . . . there is another man I've been dating," Diane finally said.

"Do you love him?" Jake asked.

"I don't know. I just don't know. He's kind and attentive and, and he's a good man, a dependable man."

"But do you love him?"

"I don't know," Diane shivered a little. "Kind of chilly, isn't it?"

Jake moved closer to her, put his arm around her for warmth. "Is that better?"

"A little," she said as she looked over at him then away.

"Is that better," he said as he gently guided her gaze back to his.

"I don't know," Diane started to say as their gazes locked and their lips tenderly touched. Diane closed her eyes and reveled in the touch of his lips on hers. Gently he pulled away. She opened her eyes and stared into his.

"I don't know," she said again and reached over to touch his face and gently guide his lips back to hers. Just then they were startled by a loud sound of honking and flapping as a bunch of geese that had been gathering in the marsh suddenly took to flight and rose up en masse over their heads. They both jumped and knocked over the thermos of cider.

"What was that?" Jake asked as Diane pointed to the geese flying in formation above.

"We must be closer to the marsh than I thought," Diane said as she stood up to look at the birds. "That's the other reason I like fall. I love watching the birds gathering as they prepare to fly south. It's such a beautiful sight."

"Tell me about it," Jake said ruefully as he stood up and brushed the leaves and brush off of his jeans. "Here, I'll see what I can salvage from our picnic." He picked up the knocked over thermos then packed away the remnants of food.

"Don't worry about it," Diane said as she got down on her knees to help. Their hands touched as they both reached into the basket, then their eyes met once again as they smiled and kissed. This time their lips slid together as readily and easily as their hands. They held the kiss even through another volley of honking overhead.

"Come on," Diane smiled as their lips parted. "Let's go see where they are all coming from." They finished packing the basket then walked hand in hand across the meadow back to the path. They spent the rest of the afternoon watching as the flocks of geese gathered and took off flying in formation above.

After the nature reserve, they stopped at a rustic restaurant on the way home to get warmed up and something to eat. A fireplace burned in the dining area and a moose head hung from the wall. Diane wrapped her hands for warmth around the large crock of hot soup she had ordered and munched on the different crackers, breadsticks and cheese that had come with their meal.

Warmed by the fire and soup and good conversation, they drove back into the city.

"I suppose you want me to drop you off at the Army?" Diane stated as she drove into the heart of the city.

"Yes, I do have some work to finish up," Jake said.

Don't spoil the day by asking about where he lives, Diane told herself over and over again. Don't spoil the day. Just hold onto the day, she told herself as she pulled into a parking space.

"Thank you for today," Jake said as he prepared to get out of the car. "I had a really nice time."

"So did I." Diane so wanted to kiss him again, to reach across the bucket seats and feel the touch of his lips on hers, but he was already out the door. "Wait," she called, "when will I see you again?"

"I'll call you," he said with a grin and a wave of his hand.

I'll call you, Diane thought as she drove back home. This man is exasperating. He can be so, so . . . special, so different and yet so infuriating. She didn't know what to think.

Michael wasn't home when she got back to the apartment. "Out with friends," she read the note he had left. "Won't be too late." There was a call from John on the answering machine.

"Hi, Diane. Got home earlier than I expected. Thought we could get together tonight. Call me." Oh dear, John. What was she to do about John? There was no way she wanted to deal with him tonight. She wanted to savor every bit of the day, her time with Jake. What was she going to say to John? At least Jake knew about John. How could she tell John about Jake?

She placed her hand on the receiver and prepared to place the phone call when the phone rang.

"Hello," she answered.

"Diane, you're home. Good. I've just got to see you. Can I come over?"

"Right now?"

"Yes, right now. I'll be over in twenty minutes."

"But John," Diane began to say only to hear the receiver be hung up. What do I do now, Diane thought?

True to his word, John was there in twenty minutes. He was clearly excited about something.

"The best news," he said as he walked in the door. "I've got great news. I've been offered a promotion."

"Oh, that's great John," Diane tried to work up some enthusiasm.

"It's even better. I'll have to move but I've worked it out so you can move with me. I'll be working in corporate headquarters out in L.A. and you can manage one of the stores in L.A."

"John," Diane started.

"Well, not right away. You'll have to start out as assistant manager, but there's room for growth and plenty of other opportunities, if not managing a store then at headquarters with me. What do you think?"

"What do I think? That's great for you. It's a great opportunity and all, but for me, I don't know. I'm not sure I want to move again so soon," Diane said hesitantly.

"That's the other great news. If you're worried about moving alone," he walked over closer to her, "you don't have to." He pulled out a small box. "You can go as my wife." He opened the box to show a sparkling diamond.

"John, it's beautiful," Diane said as she backed away, "but I can't accept it. I can't."

"I know it's rather sudden, but you know how I feel about you. I don't want to make this move alone. I want someone, you, by my side, all the way. I was going to wait until Christmas to ask you but then this job offer came along. Won't you consider it?" He pressed the ring box into her hand.

"John, I just can't accept it. I really can't." She gave the box back and turned aside.

"It's too soon. I'm sorry. If you're not ready, I'll wait. I will. It's just I'm not getting any younger and I'm ready," John paused. "I'm sorry, Diane. Maybe I got carried away with the idea. I should have waited, given you more time." He tried to take her into his arms but she resisted.

"John, I just don't know. I can't answer you tonight. I can't take this ring."

"Then don't take it for now, but please think about it, won't you? Promise me you'll think about it. Tonight doesn't have to be the final answer."

Diane looked down at the floor. How could she look him in the eyes? Finally she looked back up. "All right. I'll think about it. I will. Just not tonight. Not tonight, John."

"You're right. I never should have sprung this on you so soon. Not like this. I'm sorry. Can I see you tomorrow?"

"I'll call you, okay?"

John reluctantly let himself out of the apartment after a brief kiss on her cheek. That was all that Diane would allow.

What am I to do now, Diane thought. What a mess. She had to tell John there was someone else in her life. This had definitely gone too far. She should have known, should have recognized the warning signs. What was she to do now? Jake. She had to see Jake. But how was she to get a hold of him? How could she find him?

She thought about seeing if he was still at the Salvation Army but decided against that. She was too tired. It had been a long day. Besides what would she say to him – "John wants me to marry him and move to L.A.? What should I do?" Should she ask him what his intentions were? They still hardly knew each other. Should she give up John for this uncertain relationship with an uncertain man? She had to see him again, but then what? This too could wait for the morning.

It was late when Michael got home that night. Even though she had not waited up for him she had been awake, tossing and turning. She thought about asking him where he had been, but thought better of it. Why add one more worry to an already long day? She heard Michael go into the refrigerator, get something to eat. Eventually she thought she heard him turning out the light in the bedroom. Finally she fell into a fitful sleep.

Chapter 9

This was not a morning to miss church, she decided. So despite her fitful sleep, she got up and quietly let herself out of the apartment in order to go to the ten o'clock service. She had decided to let Michael sleep. There would be time enough to interrogate him as to why he was so late last night when she got back.

It felt good going to church. She was slowly getting to know more people at this church, but she mostly kept to herself. The music was comforting and the sermon, while not always speaking to her, still had something in it that she could chew on, think and pray about. It was somewhat familiar in this rapidly changing world she was living in. Today's sermon had been on Paul's quote for Romans, "All things work for the good for those who love God." She didn't know how this particular mess was going to work out, but she kept reassuring herself that somehow it would work for the best and she would know what to do.

When she got home there was a message on her answering machine from John. "Sorry again about last night. Let's just forget the whole thing, at least for now. Call me."

"What is that all about?" Michael asked as he walked out of his room.

"Nothing, John just wants me to marry him and move to L.A."

"What! And what about me? What am I supposed to do?" Michael went ballistic on her.

"I didn't say yes. I wouldn't do something like that without talking to you."

"Sure you wouldn't, like you wouldn't sell our house and force me to leave my friends."

"That was different, Michael. I thought we've been through this. I'm not marrying John and I'm not moving to L.A., at least not right now." That was of little comfort to Michael. "Besides which, where were you so late last night?" Diane asked.

"With my friends, what few friends I have."

"Well, why don't you invite them over? Why can't I meet them?"

"Sure, Mom, I'm sure they're interested in meeting my mom. And what about your new friends? When do I get to meet them?

What about this Jake guy? Does John know about him? Is that where you were yesterday?" Michael glared at her.

"That's different."

"Why is it different, Mom?"

"Look, Michael, let's just drop this conversation. It's getting us nowhere and we may end up saying something we don't mean."

"Sure, Mom, whatever you say, Mom. I'm going out." Michael grabbed his jacket and walked out.

"Michael, wait," Diane shouted back at him but he was already gone. Just like his father, she thought. How like his father. He just wanted an excuse to leave. She knew that but it still hurt terribly. Now I've got to see Jake, she thought to herself. The phone rang. It was John again. She let the machine take the call while she left the apartment.

There wasn't anyone at the Salvation Army as far as she could tell. She told herself she should have known Jake wouldn't be in to work till later. Still she knocked on the doors and windows hoping to catch someone's attention.

"Can I help you," an older gentleman tapped her on the shoulder. She jumped then calmed herself and said, "I was looking for someone who works here."

"Maybe I can help you. Who are you looking for?"

"Jake Alexander."

"Sure I know Jake, but he won't be around till much later today."

"Do you have any idea how I might reach him? It's real important."

"Well, yeah, I think I know where he lives. He doesn't let on to too many about where he lives. Likes his privacy, I guess, but I can take you there."

"Would you? I'd be so grateful."

"Sure thing, ma'am. Happy to help you." Diane walked several blocks with the man who introduced himself to her as Harry. Finally they came to an apartment building. It wasn't as rundown as some in the neighborhood, seemed relatively clean. Harry pointed out the building. "I'm not sure which apartment he lives in but I'm pretty sure it's in that building. Hey," he shouted to a kid sitting on the front steps. "Do you know Jake Alexander?"

"Sure I do. What's it to you?"

"Can you tell me which apartment is his?"

"I can take you to it."

"Thanks. This lady is looking for him." He turned to Diane. "I guess this is where we part company. It's been a pleasure."

Diane followed her new escort up two flights of stairs to the third floor apartment at the end of the hall. He knocked loudly on the door and hollered, "Jake, someone here to see you."

"Coming," Diane could hear his voice from within the room. "Hey, Sammy," Jake said as he opened the door, then looked with surprise at Diane. "Diane. How'd you find this place?"

"Fellow named Harry walked me here then this young man was kind enough to escort me the rest of the way. I hope it's all right, my coming here."

"No, it's fine, come in. Thanks Sam," he said and rubbed the young boy's head.

"Any time, Jake," Sam said as he left.

"I'm afraid it's not much," Jake said as he picked up some clothes lying about and cleared off a chair for her. It was a small, one room efficiency. Jake quickly made the bed into a couch and finished making the room more presentable. "I wasn't expecting company," he explained as he tidied the room.

"I'm sorry, but I didn't have a phone number to call."

"I don't have a phone. Just an unnecessary expense. I get messages at the Army and the soup kitchen. People, if they need to get a hold of me, they generally know how to do it."

"Like me."

"Like you. Would you like a cup of coffee or tea or something?"

"Tea would be nice." Diane sat down at the small table in the kitchen area of the apartment. Neither talked as Jake fussed about heating water for tea. Diane looked around the simple room. No phone, no TV, no stereo, a radio tuned to a classical music station sat on an end table. There was the sofa-bed, one easy chair, a dresser, a table with a lamp on it and a few books. That was the extent of the furniture and décor. The kitchen was sparsely furnished. No microwave, just a toaster oven. Jake was heating water in a tea kettle on the stove. A small refrigerator was the only other appliance. It was simple, bare and clean.

Jake poured hot water into a cup and dunked a tea bag into it
several times before giving it to her. "Sugar?" he asked.

"No, thank you," she said. He fixed a cup for himself and sat
down across from her.

"I'm afraid it's not much, but it's home. It's all I really need.
Sorry about yesterday . . ." he began.

"Yesterday was very nice," Diane said.

"Yes, I know it was. I just hope I didn't give you the wrong
idea," he said apologetically.

"What wrong idea?" she asked.

"I mean, I don't want to mislead you. I mean, I like you a lot,
but as you can see, I haven't got much. I realize I don't really have
any business going out with someone like you. What can I offer you
but a cup of tea?"

"And a kind word. That's all I want right now. A kind word."

"What's wrong?"

"Everything. You know John, the man I told you about
yesterday?"

"Yes, the one you didn't know whether you loved."

"He wants me to marry him."

"Oh," Jake turned sideways in his chair. After a pause he said,
"And what did you say?"

"I said I didn't know."

"So why don't you know?"

"Well, I thought . . . I thought, maybe you and me . . ." Diane
stood up, "obviously I was being very foolish, wasn't I? I thought
just maybe there was something between you and me. I guess I was
wrong. Thank you for the tea. I guess I should go."

"Wait, don't go." He took her hand and had her sit back down.
"I hate to drink alone." He shuffled his feet under the table then said.
"Look, Diane, I'm real sorry about yesterday."

"I'm not," Diane said.

"But don't you see how I live? I had no business taking up with
someone like you. You deserve better. You deserve someone who
can provide nice things for you. Someone you can depend on. Not
someone like me. You said it yourself, you don't think you can
depend on me. This is my life. I'm not going to change. It's no life
for you. It's kind of like a ministry I've got here. A street ministry. I
look out for those who can't look out for themselves. This is my way

of making amends for all the ways in which I've blown it in my life."

He paused as he worried how his words might be affecting her. "But now I've blown it again. I never meant for it to go any farther than just friendship. I don't know what I was doing, and then yesterday, I just had to kiss you, but it was wrong. If you love John, then marry him. You deserve to be married, but I'm not the marrying kind. I've been down that road before. I'm not going again."

"Oh, I see, I see all right. You think so little of me that you think all I care about is money."

"That's not it, Diane."

"No, you're right, it isn't. You're just scared."

"You don't understand."

"I guess I don't." Diane sat feeling very confused, then she stood up. "I guess there's nothing else for me to do but leave then."

"I guess that's right, but, if you need me, you know how to get a hold of me, don't you?"

"Sure, sure. In an emergency you'll be there, but don't call otherwise. In other words, don't need me, don't depend on me to be there, because I won't be. Seems I've heard those words before. At least this time I didn't make the mistake of marrying you," Diane said as she walked to the door.

"Diane, wait, don't go like this," Jake said.

"How else should I go? Leave me my dignity," Diane said as she walked out the door. She managed to find her way back through the unfamiliar streets to her car as she willed away the tears welling in her eyes. She wouldn't waste any tears on Jake. At least now she knew the answer for John. It was going to work out for the best, wasn't it? She told herself that as she drove home. All things work for good for those who love God.

Chapter 10

Diane didn't tell John yes, but she also didn't tell him no. She told him she needed more time. He had to move to Los Angeles by December. They agreed to spend Thanksgiving each with their own families and that he would move to Los Angeles without her. Diane felt she needed the space not only to think but also for the children. She wanted to give them time to adjust to the changes that had already happened before springing any new changes. She and her children, she thought, needed the "normalcy" of a Thanksgiving in her hometown with her parents, if that could be called normal.

Michael was happy to be back with his friends. Adrian was happy not to be spending Thanksgiving in a cramped apartment. Diane was happy to be away from John and the need to make a decision. She was happy to be away from the city and her new life. It was a comfortable retreat for her from all the changes and new directions her life was taking. And Thanksgiving was usually a pleasant time with her parents. There weren't the same heavy demands that accompanied Christmas. All it entailed was one meal together. She could handle that.

Michael got to spend some time with Tom's parents. It was pleasant to see them again. Despite her divorce she had remained on good terms with her former in-laws. It was also a good opportunity for her and Marge to catch up on each other's lives over lunch that Friday.

"Of all the weekends for you to come home, you had to pick Thanksgiving and thereby rob me of the excuse to go to the city for the biggest shopping day of the year."

"Oh, come on, Marge. You're not missing anything and you know it. You're missing crowds and traffic."

"Yes, but just once I'd like to say I did it."

"Besides, you don't need an excuse to go to the 'city.' You've got me. Isn't that excuse enough?"

"Right you are. So tell me, how goes it with all the men in your life?"

"You mean the man in my life, John."

"But what about the mysterious Jake?"

"Oh, that? That was nothing."

"Don't tell me that it was nothing when I know that's not the truth. I can tell when you are lying."

"It's nothing. It's over. It never really began. He called it off. He's not interested in a relationship. It's that simple."

"I'm sorry to hear that. I liked him even though I didn't know him. A mystery man."

"There's no mystery to him. He's not interested in becoming involved with any woman, much less me. He's too busy with his 'work' such as it is."

"Hmmm, there's more to it than that, I can tell. But if you're not willing tell your best friend . . ." Marge leaned forward, pushing back the brown waves that framed her face, encouraging Diane to spill what was really going on with her.

"There's nothing to tell."

"All right, all right. I'll drop the subject. So what about John?" She leaned back in her chair.

"He's asked me to marry him."

"Whoa, he doesn't waste any time."

"Well, he's being transferred to Los Angeles. He wants me to come with him."

"And move so far from me, no way. I knew there was a reason I didn't like him. If this is so serious, how come you are not spending Thanksgiving together?"

"Because it isn't that serious. I'm not really ready to make such a move or take such a step. I told him I needed more time. Besides there's Michael."

"So what does Michael think of all of this?"

"I don't know. He seemed to like John okay at first but now he doesn't want to have anything to do with him. He's not impolite, but he avoids John whenever he comes over. I don't know what to think."

"It's only normal that he be threatened by a man in your life."

"But it's more than that. I'm not sure what is going on with Michael. He seemed so much better at first when he moved back but now he's just as uncommunicative as ever. Between school, his after school job and his friends, I hardly ever see him."

"Sounds pretty normal to me for someone his age."

"Yeah, but there's something going on. The other day he asked about his father. He hasn't said a word about his father for nine years."

"I don't think it's strange that he wants to know more about his dad. What's strange is that he hasn't asked before this."

"He used to ask a lot, those first years after Tom left. But not since that time he tried to run away and find him. I'm not sure what happened but he hasn't asked about Tom since then."

"Then maybe that's a good sign. It's only natural that he would want to know about his dad."

"Yeah, I guess so," Diane paused as she sipped her coffee. Then she put the cup down, reached for the bill and said, "We can't let the biggest shopping day of the year pass us by. Let's go see what we can find here." They spent the rest of the afternoon visiting the local stores, picking out odds and ends for Christmas before going their separate ways.

John called that night. They had talked briefly the night before. John had been spending Thanksgiving with his family at his oldest son's home. It had been noisy and crowded. There had been little privacy to talk so the conversation had been short. Now he was back home for the weekend.

"I miss you," John said as she picked up the receiver of the phone in her parent's bedroom where she had gone for privacy.

"With all those people around?" Diane had quipped.

"They're not around anymore, but even when they were, I still missed you."

"So how is everybody?" Diane avoided saying anything about missing him. She did and she didn't. She kind of missed him, but she was also glad he wasn't around. She wondered what would happen once he moved. Would she completely forget about him? What chance did their relationship really have?

Jake, on the other hand, she was having a hard time forgetting. Perhaps it was the lure of the forbidden fruit. She didn't know why, she just knew he continued to be on her mind no matter how much she tried to free herself of thoughts of him. It was almost as bad as all those years she had spent trying to put Tom out of her mind. She had succeeded then, certainly she could succeed now. After all, Tom had been her husband, her first love. Jake she had hardly known. She could easily dismiss him from her mind. Still memories of him kept coming back to her when least expected. She had never said anything to John about him. What was there to tell anyway? Nothing, nothing had happened and nothing was going to happen. In the meantime, she continued to be concerned about Michael.

Michael seemed so much better this weekend. He was genuinely happy to be here. He spent a good part of Friday at Tom's parents. They had always been cordial, but not close. Diane wondered about this new found interest in his grandparents.

Adrian had not stayed through the weekend. She had said she had too many exams to prepare for and papers to write so she had returned to college. Diane had wondered how much studying was actually going on but kept this to herself. By Saturday evening she was wishing she had gone back early like John. It was good to see her parents, good to visit, but the quarters were a little too close for comfort. She was anxious to get back to her own space.

Her mom had inquired about the man who had called her. She had not said anything to her parents about John yet. Her mom was pleased to know there was finally another man in her life. She had not felt good about this daughter, raising two children on her own without the help of a man, and now living in that city! She was happy to think her daughter might finally have a man to look after her.

"He's just a friend, Mom. No big deal," Diane had said.

"No big deal," Michael had commented, "he only wants to marry her." Diane gave Michael one of her looks then groaned internally as she heard the expected barrage of questions.

"Diane, that's wonderful. What does he do for a living? When do we get to meet him?"

"You'll get to meet him when and if I decide this is serious, okay, Mom," Diane tried to ward off any more questions.

"Julie, leave her alone. She'll let you know when she's good and ready, isn't that right, honey?" her dad had intervened on her behalf, coming to her assistance like he had so often in her teens. Diane shot him a grateful smile while her mother continued to fuss and complain under her breath as she cleaned the dishes from the table.

Diane breathed a sigh of relief when they pulled out of the driveway the next day. "It was nice to visit but I'll be glad to get home," she said to Michael.

"Yeah. It's a nice place to visit but I wouldn't want to live there anymore."

"Precisely," she smiled. She was happy to see Michael in such a good mood. This visit had done him some good.

"Mom," Michael began tentatively. Diane knew that tone of voice, knew he was about to ask something. She wondered what.

"Yes?"

"How come you never talk about Dad?"

"Your father?"

"Yes, my father. How come? And don't give me that strained look."

"What look?"

"The look you always get on your face any time anyone mentions his name in your presence." She could feel Michael's gaze upon her face.

"That look? I didn't realize I had one."

"You do. Why do you think I never asked about him before?"

"Because it was in the past and you had moved on?"

"No, because you always got that strained look on your face that told me it wasn't okay to bring the subject up."

Diane was grateful for the need to keep her eyes focused on the road. She knew Michael was looking intently at her. She didn't want to see the expression on his face. "Oh, I'm sorry if I did that. I didn't mean to. It's just, I don't know, it was hard for me to talk to anyone about your dad for a long time. When you kids stopped asking about him, I thought maybe that was the case for you, too, so I didn't want to bring him up."

"He wasn't dead."

"I know, but I think that made it harder. If he were dead, it was understandable that he never wrote or inquired about you kids."

"What was he like? I remember so little about him."

Diane felt sad thinking about Tom even after all of these years. "He was a good man, Michael, just so young. We both were so young when we got married. We didn't have any idea what we were doing. Your dad really wasn't ready for all of the responsibility of raising a family, but then, how many of us really are ready?"

"Was it that bad for you?"

"Not at first. We were young and in love. We thought we could do anything. I thought your dad could do anything. He was so full of dreams. Then Adrian was born. We had so many expenses. And then you were born. Your dad started to drink more and more . . ." her voice trailed off momentarily, "and then he left. He said he was going to send for us, but I knew he wouldn't. He was always such a dreamer. Reality could never keep up with his dreams. He was never satisfied. Always wanted something more. Always chasing after something, but I don't know what. I hope he got it."

"It must have been very hard for you?"

"Yes, it was, but I had you two kids. I had to keep going for your sakes if nothing else. Part of me wanted to believe him, wanted to believe he would come back. But another part knew he wouldn't." Diane focused on the road ahead. "But that's all over and done with. It's in the past. He's gone, but I've got you and Adrian. You are good kids, both of you. I've been blessed."

"Mom, what if I tell you I want to see Dad?"

"But nobody knows where he is. He hasn't written, hasn't kept in touch with anyone, not even his own parents."

"But that's it. I want to know. Is he even alive? If he is alive, I want to see him."

"How are you going to do that?"

"Grandpa said he would help me. We're going to hire a detective."

"But we did that years ago."

"But that was years ago. Maybe they can find something now. I'm going to do this. I have to do this. I just wanted you to know."

"Thank you, Michael. Thank you for telling me," Diane said. "And if I can help, let me know."

"I will, Mom. I sure will." They drove the rest of the way home in silence.

Chapter 11

It's funny how sometimes the mere mention of someone from your past can awaken such strong memories and feelings, almost as if no time had passed. That was how she had felt when Michael had brought up that he was trying to find his dad. Memories and feelings she had thought she had put behind her came storming back. Conflicting memories. Memories of the good times and the not so good times. Memories of the last time she had seen him. Memories of that last phone call, promising he'd send for her and the kids. She had thought she had dealt with those feelings. Thought they were gone only to have them resurface when she least expected them.

She was relieved when Michael didn't bring up the subject again. She hoped he had forgotten, although in her heart she knew he hadn't. His silence didn't mean he wasn't looking. It just meant he hadn't found him yet. And then what happens, Diane wondered. Would he just dance back into their lives, into the lives of all three of them? Her life and the lives of their son and daughter? How would it be? Would he be changed? She had changed. What if he told Michael he never wanted to see him again? Anything could happen.

She had no control over the events and so tried to put it out of her mind, hope for the best and pray. Pray with all of her might. And maybe this time she'd get an answer. She was afraid even to acknowledge the thought. After so many years of silence, she had become accustomed to it. She no longer expected answers, but she prayed just the same. It was a source of comfort to her in a troubling, confusing world.

She focused on her job, her employees, her customers. To a lesser extent she focused on John. He had moved at the beginning of December. He called faithfully, still out of sight, out of mind. She was relieved not to have to think too much about him. She wished she could have said the same about Jake. Out of sight did not mean out of mind where he was concerned. She struggled to make it so, only to have thoughts of him come creeping back into her consciousness. She tried replacing those thoughts with ones of John, but this didn't work either. She didn't know what to do.

Fortunately the store was keeping her very busy with all of the Christmas rush and need for extra hours and extra employees. And after Christmas there would be end-of-year sales and inventory. She could keep herself busy with all of that, she told herself. Michael seemed to be doing okay in school and at work. She didn't see him that much but when she did he seemed to be fine, in good spirits. She was grateful for that. She had many reasons to count her blessings as the holidays approached.

"Whatever happened to that female friend of yours – Diane, I believe was her name?" Esther finally cornered Jake to ask.

"Nothing happened."

"Then how come she doesn't come around?"

"Because nothing happened, she's just a friend."

"That's not how I saw it. The way she looked at you, that was more than a friend. Child, isn't it about time you had a woman in your life? What is it with this monk's existence?"

"I'm just waiting for you," Jake teased.

"Just say the word, blue eyes, and I'm yours," Esther teased back as she went back to washing dishes, shaking her head.

It's not that Jake didn't think about Diane, more than he should, he told himself. It just wasn't a good idea. There wasn't any room for a woman in his life, not now, maybe never. He was happy with his life the way it was. Why complicate things with a relationship? He liked her just fine right now, but if he were to get involved she'd probably start trying to change him the way women always did. What woman would be content living life the way he did? She'd want a nicer place to live, stability and a better paying job. He'd want that too, if he were to marry again. But he didn't deserve that, he thought.

He had had that once and he had given it up. He didn't regret giving it up. So what right did he have now to have those things again? What right did he have to a relationship, a family? What right did he have to mess up another woman's life? He'd messed up his own enough. He didn't need to mess up anybody else's. Guilt was not a pleasant companion but it was a companion. Besides, he was happy with his life. He was making a difference. Here he was able to help others if only in a small way. He was shaken out of his reverie by someone calling his name.

"Jake, this young man is looking for you," one of the volunteers at the soup kitchen called out as he sent a lanky teenager in Jake's direction.

"Hi, you Jake Alexander?" the teen asked.

"Last time I checked I was. How can I help you?"

"I'm trying to locate someone. I was told at the Salvation Army that you know a lot of people on the street and might be able to help me."

"I might. Who are you looking for?" Jake stared into the young man's eyes, eyes that seemed familiar.

"This is the only picture I have, but it's almost twenty years old. It's my dad. Tom Price. I'm trying to find him." Jake started inside at the name. Could this be Michael, he thought.

"And your name?"

"It's Michael, Michael Price," Michael extended his hand.

"Pleased to meet you, Michael," Jake said as he shook his hand. "I believe I know your mother, Diane."

Michael looked surprised then said, "Are you the Jake from the answering machine?"

"I'm afraid I am."

"You're not how I thought you'd be."

"How'd you think I would be?" Jake looked Michael up and down. He was the way Jake had thought he would be. His mother's brown eyes and auburn hair. Must be his father's jaw, though, Jake thought.

"I thought you'd be another one of those stuffed shirts my mom works with. You know, management types from the store who always wear a shirt and tie." Michael sized Jake up as well. He wasn't sure, but he thought he liked what he saw.

"That I'm not."

"I see that. How'd you meet my mother?"

"Long story. Let's just say we met by chance."

"You haven't called in a while."

"Another long story. Look, about your dad, what makes you think I might know him?"

"I had a detective looking for him. The last trace of him was that he was here somewhere in the city, but that was five years ago. He seems to have disappeared since then. I thought that, maybe, if he was living on the street somewhere the people at the Salvation Army might have seen him, and they sent me to you.”

“How long has it been since you last saw him?”

“Over thirteen years. I was five when he left.”

“That’s a long time for someone to be missing. Don’t you think that if he wanted to be found, he would have been by now?” Jake started taking chairs off the tables and set them up for the evening meal.

“Look, if you don’t want to help me just say so. Don’t give me a lecture.” Michael put the picture back in his pocket and prepared to leave.

“Wait a minute,” Jake stopped what he was doing and grabbed him by the arm. “Let me see the picture again.” After looking carefully at it Jake handed it back. “I don’t recognize him right off, but I will keep an eye out for him. I’ll also ask around for him. Fair enough?”

“Fair enough, thank you,” Michael said with relief. “This is really important to me.”

“I can see that. How do I get a hold of you? Do you want me to call at your home?”

“No, no don’t. I’ll contact you. Or you can contact me at my job. I work at . . .”

“The Stop and Go. Your mom told me about it.”

“What else did she tell you?” Michael asked suspiciously.

“Just that you were a good kid and that she loved you.”

“Right,” Michael responded. “I work most afternoons after school. You can always reach me there.”

“Will do, and Michael,” Jake reached over and shook his hand again. “It was nice meeting you. I mean it. I hope I can help.”

“Yeah,” Michael said as he walked off, not sure how to respond. At least he was willing to help but Michael wondered about Jake’s relationship with his mother. He thought there was more to it but didn’t know what.

Jake had been surprised by Michael’s visit. He wondered if Diane knew what her son was doing. He wondered if he should tell her, or was he just looking for an excuse to see her again? He wasn’t sure he could trust his motives.

Jake didn’t recognize the picture, but then twenty years, especially if some of them had been spent on the street, definitely changed someone. Trying to find someone who had disappeared in this city five years ago, what was the chance of that happening? Especially if the person did not want to be found. He certainly knew about that. What made this kid think he could succeed where a detective hadn't? He must be pretty desperate, Jake thought.

He wondered about his own sons. Were they as interested in finding him? He highly doubted it. After all, they had been older when he had left. He doubted his ex-wife had done anything to "preserve" his memory. No, no chance they'd be looking him up in the near future. Still he wondered about them, especially his daughter who would be graduating this year. How he'd like to see that, if only she wouldn't spit in his face. That's probably what his ex would do, but not his daughter. Would she do that? Had she found it in her to forgive him yet? He wondered. Maybe there was nothing he could do for his own children, at least he could try to help Michael, he told himself.

Chapter 12

Diane sat in the quiet of her apartment and stared out the windows to the street below. Her cat was curled up in her lap, purring contentedly. Michael was at work. John was in L.A. She was alone with her thoughts. What trees she could see from her window were stripped bare of leaves. She felt barren and empty as well. So much of her life had been stripped away over that past year leaving her exposed and vulnerable. She didn't know what to do.

The scripture passages at church this morning seemed to be such a contrast to her mood, readings of joyful expectancy as they prepared for Christmas. They only made her feel worse as she contrasted her own feelings to those of everybody else, or at least what she perceived to be the feelings of those around her. Certainly she was not alone in finding the holiday season a trying time.

Her preoccupation with her work helped some to hold off the emptiness, but now, sitting alone in her apartment there was no hiding from her feelings. She could go out. She could call a friend, go shopping. But no, she needed to be where she was. She needed to face what was going on inside of her.

The thought of Christmas brought her no joy. John wanted her to spend it with him. Adrian had reluctantly agreed to come home for Christmas day, but she let her know that it would be a short stay at most. Adrian had plans for the holidays that didn't include family. Diane suspected those plans did include a new boyfriend. She hoped this one might work out for her. Apparently she wasn't ready to invite him "home" with her for Christmas, not that Adrian considered this apartment home. Still it was home for Diane. She didn't know what Michael thought about it. He was home so rarely these days. He was working a lot of hours and checking out leads on where his dad might be. Michael wasn't talking to her about it, but she suspected that was where he was at times.

Perhaps this was just her usual Christmas slump. She usually had one at some point each holiday season. It was hard to keep up with so much good cheer and holiday spirit. Sometimes she just had to rebel and feel miserable for a while.

She tried not to think about Jake. The thought of him just left her feeling emptier and more alone. It was good to be alone at times.

She was good company for herself. Why did this man have to come into her life and open up old wounds without even knowing he was doing it? Why had he showed up in her life now? Was there a reason? She sure didn't know.

She wondered how Michael's search for his dad was going but was afraid to ask. She didn't really want to know. Instead she sat, staring at the barren trees and feeling barren herself. She was wishing for a light coating of snow to cover over her, blanket her with warmth and shield her from harm. She longed to sleep under a blanket of cool white snow, she thought as she slouched back and began to nod off. She was jarred awake by the sound of the phone. She fumbled for the phone, just barely beating her answering machine to the call.

"Hello?" she said.

"Mom, it's me. Can you come right away?" she heard Michael's familiar voice.

"Where are you? What's wrong? Are you in trouble?" she asked.

"No, Mom, I'm fine, but I found Dad. I found out where he is. I need your help."

"Where are you now?"

"I'm at the hospital. Can you meet me here?"

"Of course. I'll be there as soon as I can. Which one? St. Lawrence? Where is that?" Diane wrote down the name and address.

"Thanks. I'll be in the lobby. I'll explain it all then."

Diane hung up the phone. Could this day get any worse, she thought. No wonder she had been in such a foul mood, a mood of foreboding. But no time to think about that now, now was a time for action. Her son needed her. She had to go. She grabbed her winter coat and car keys and headed for the door.

She drove as carefully as possibly, despite her racing mind. Tom, Michael had found Tom. Was he hurt? Was he alive? How? These thoughts kept running through her head.

Michael met her in the lobby as he had promised. Behind him stood Jake, of all people. She had been expecting to see Tom. Instead she saw Jake.

"What is it, Michael? What's going on?"

"Hi, Mom. You remember Jake? He's been helping me find Dad."

Diane gave Jake a puzzled look. "I'll explain it later," his eyes seemed to say as Michael took her by the hand and led her down the hall, explaining all the while. Jake followed behind.

"He's been in an accident, actually I guess it was a bar fight. He's in intensive care, but they won't let me see him. Say I have to have proof that I'm next of kin. I thought maybe you could help. Oh, and he's changed his name to Wright.

"Wright? Michael, are you sure you've got the right man?"

"No, that's another reason why I need you to help me identify him."

Michael led her to the intensive care unit. She tried to tell the nurse she was his wife only to be told his wife had just been notified and was on her way. "His ex-wife, I meant to say, or at least I think I am." The nurse gave her a patronizing look and prepared to escort her out the door.

"I'm sorry, ma'am. Only next of kin are allowed in. You'll have to wait in the waiting room."

"But I am next of kin. I'm his son," Michael stated.

"We just talked to his wife and she didn't say anything about a son. Now if you will please move along." She took Diane by the arm.

Jake stepped forward and took the nurse's hand off of Diane's arm. "If you would just listen for a minute. We believe this man may be her former husband whom she hasn't seen for thirteen years. If so, this young man is his son."

"Even if that is the case, this is not the time and place for a family reunion. It's likely to be too upsetting to the patient."

"Couldn't we please, couldn't she take a look at him through the window to know whether we even have the right man. Please." Jake turned on his charm and finally the nurse agreed.

"All right, but you mustn't try to talk to him. Just look and see if it's him then leave."

"That's what I'll do," Diane reassured the nurse.

"You can go with her but the young man has to stay here," the nurse told Jake.

"But," Michael began to complain. Jake placed his hand firmly on Michael's shoulder and reassured him.

"Don't worry. It's probably better this way. Let your mother identify him first then we'll go from there."

"All right," Michael reluctantly agreed. Jake took Diane by the hand and guided her through the maze of ICU, following after the nurse. Diane's heart was pounding and her head was swimming. She walked through the maze of machines, nurses and equipment in a daze. Finally they stopped. Diane looked through the window at the man lying quietly surrounded by tubes and monitors. She grabbed hold of Jake for support. Could it really be him? Underneath all those wires was that her Tom? If only he would open his eyes. The man slowly opened his eyes and groggily called for help. She knew that voice. It had to be him. Tears filled her eyes as Jake slowly led her away.

"Was it?" he asked gently.

"Yes. It had to be him. Older but still him. It was his voice." Michael was anxiously waiting their return.

"Was it him, Mom? Was it?"

"Yes," she said.

"You still can't go in to see him," the nurse insisted.

"Let's go into another room," Jake suggested. "Come on, Michael, I think your mother needs some water." Jake gently led both of them into the waiting room. Jake got Diane some water while she sat down, visibly shaken.

"Why can't I see him? I've waited so long," Michael started.

"And you can wait a little longer. Can't you see your mother's in a state? Besides that, do you really think it would be good for your dad to see you right now, after all these years, while he's in critical condition? How do you think that will affect him?"

"I don't know. I guess, I'm just afraid of his slipping away again without me seeing him."

"Don't worry, Michael, that man isn't going anywhere for a while. There will be time enough to talk to him."

"But what's wrong with him? What if he dies and I never get to talk to him?"

"I'll check with the nurse about his status. Right now you stay with your mother." Michael paced nervously about the room while Diane drank the glass of water Jake had given her. She was still in shock from seeing Tom after so many years and under such circumstances. She was glad he hadn't seen her. Was glad she had spared him that.

"What did they say?" Michael jumped on Jake as soon as he returned.

"Just a minute, young man. Can't you see your mother needs some attention right now?" He went over and sat next to Diane. He took the cup of water from her and held her hand in both of his.

"Are you okay?" he asked.

"I'm fine, just shaken. How is he?"

"Well, the nurse says she can't release that information to anyone but . . ."

". . . Next of kin," Diane jumped in. "I thought as much. So what do we do now?"

"She did say he was in no immediate danger," Jake reassured Michael and Diane. "It seems he has a wife. She's on her way. Maybe we'll be able to talk to her when she gets here. She might be willing to tell us something. I guess all we can do now is wait for her."

"What? That's all we can do? My father may be dying in the next room and I can't even see him. Can't talk to him? No. I can't accept this," Michael shouted.

"Michael, don't you see it's for your dad's own good he can't see you yet. The shock may be too much for him. Better to wait, see how he is, talk to his wife."

"But I'm his son. Doesn't that matter to anybody?"

"Of course it matters, Michael. It matters," Diane intervened. "You just have to be patient."

"Look, you two wait in here. I'll be on the look-out for his wife," Jake instructed them. Michael came over and sat next to Diane. She took his hand.

"I know this is hard for you," she said. "It's hard for me too."

"You have no idea how hard it is," Michael said and pulled his hand away. He propped his head into his hands and waited without speaking.

Jake watched as a tired, middle-aged woman walked down the hall into intensive care. He followed her in and waited by the door as she spoke to the nurse.

"Can I see my husband?" he heard her ask.

"Just for a little while. He's sleeping comfortably now. We don't want him disturbed."

Jake watched her walk over to the room they had stood by a short while ago. He waited until she turned around and walked back to the nurses' station.

"Mrs. Wright?" Jake approached her. She looked very tired and worn. She wore a sweater over a blouse and a tight blue skirt. Her coat was draped over her arm. Short tight curls circled her face.

"Yes," she responded, "do I know you?"

"No, you don't. Could I talk to you about your husband?"

"What kind of trouble is he in now?" she asked.

"No trouble, it's just," Jake pulled her aside, "did you know your husband's real name is Price?"

"How did you know that?" Mrs. Wright dropped her voice.

"He was also married. His former wife and his son are here. They want to see him."

"Oh," she said and paused. "They're here? Tommy never said much about his ex-wife. In fact the only way I knew he even had a family was because of the picture he keeps in his wallet. I saw it one day and asked him about her. How'd she find him?"

"She didn't. His son did. He's been trying to find him for some time."

"We don't have any money for child support."

"He's not looking for money. Just a father. How long have you been married?"

"Just four years. But they've been good ones, except for when he drinks too much. But that's not that often. Not really." Her eyes betrayed her as she looked down.

"They'd really like to see him. What did the nurses say? How is he?"

"He's not entirely out of danger, but he's holding his own. If he continues to hold his own he may be moved out of critical care in a day or two."

"Can I tell them that, Mrs. Wright? They really want to know."

"It's Sadie. You can call me Sadie."

"Sadie, is that all right?"

"Sure, that's fine. I'll tell them." Jake escorted her into the waiting room and introduced her to Michael and Diane.

Sadie awkwardly shook Diane's hand and Michael's. "You look like your dad," she told him.

"How is he? Can I see him?"

"Not right now. He's sleeping peacefully and the nurses don't want him disturbed. I'm not even supposed to be with him."

"Couldn't I just see him? Just for a minute. I won't say a word," Michael asked.

"I'm afraid that's not for me to say."

"Does he ever talk about me?"

"Well, no, he doesn't talk much about what he did before we met, but I'm sure he'd be proud of you," Sadie tried to ease the truth a little.

A nurse came in looking for Mrs. Wright.

"I'm here," Sadie said.

"Your husband is looking for you. Would you please come in and talk to him but just for a few minutes."

"Could I please see my dad?" Michael pushed forward.

"I don't . . ." the nurse began.

"Look, I won't go into the room. I just want to see him. Is that too much to ask?"

"Well, if it's all right with Mrs. Wright . . ."

"Sure," Sadie responded, "it's fine." Michael accompanied Sadie into the intensive care unit. He stood outside and looked in as Sadie spoke with Tom and calmed him down. After a while Michael went back into the waiting room. They were joined by Sadie shortly afterward.

"He's sleeping soundly now. There's nothing to do here."

"Did you tell him I was here?" Michael asked.

"No, I thought maybe I should wait till he is stronger. Why don't you go home? I can call you if anything happens."

"That sounds like a good idea, Michael. We can come back tomorrow," Diane said.

"I guess, if I have to," Michael reluctantly agreed. Jake walked out of the hospital with Diane and Michael. Michael went ahead to the car while Diane talked to Jake.

"Thank you for being here," Diane told him. "So you've been helping Michael?"

"It's a long story."

"I believe it. Thank you anyway."

"You going to be okay?"

"Yeah, I think so. I'll be fine. It's Michael I'm worried about."

"He's a good kid."

"Yeah, but still a kid."

"He'll be fine," Jake said. "Are you going to be okay?"

"Yeah. It was hard, real hard, seeing Tom again and under these circumstances, but I'll be okay." Diane attempted a smile as she avoided Jake's gaze.

"I'll call you tomorrow," Jake told her as she climbed into her car. "I want to know what's happening. Good night, Michael." Jake called across the car to Michael before leaving.

Diane and Michael drove home without speaking.

"Do you want something to eat?" Diane asked once they got home.

"No, I'm not hungry."

"You really should eat something."

"I told you, Mom, I'm not hungry," Michael snapped at her.

"You know, Michael, maybe I better talk to your dad first, before you do," Diane said tentatively.

"Sure, Mom, whatever you say," Michael replied then went to his room.

Could this day get any worse, Diane thought as she hung up her coat and started to fix something for herself to eat. She stopped what she was doing to pick up the phone. It was John.

"Is it the hospital?" Michael came out of his room to ask.

"No, Michael. It's just John." Michael went back into his room.

"Just John, I like that," John said. "What kind of a welcome is that?"

"I'm sorry, John. Michael was expecting a call. How are you?"

"I'm fine, and in town for the holidays. I got a few extra days so I thought I'd come out early. When can I see you?"

"Not tonight, John. I don't know when."

"Is this a brush-off or what?"

"No, no, it's just, it's been a really rough day. Michael has found his father. He's in the hospital."

"I'm sorry to hear that, I mean not that Michael has found his dad, but that he's in the hospital."

"Yes, I know what you mean. I don't really know what's happening. I don't know what we'll be doing for the next few days."

"Certainly you can squeeze in some time for me."

"I'll try, John. I really will."

There was a pause on the phone, finally John said, "It's okay. You do what you have to do. I am a patient man but . . ."

"I know it's a lot to ask. I'll call you as soon as things have settled down a little more here."

"Please do. Let me know if I can help."

"I will," Diane said and hung up the phone. Yet another complication for a complicated situation, Diane thought to herself. What was she to do? She heated some soup and hot water for tea then went to bed as soon as she finished eating, exhausted from the day's events.

Chapter 13

She slept fitfully throughout the night but at least she did sleep. Her dreams were filled with strange images. She kept thinking she heard the phone ring only to wake and realize it had just been a dream. When her alarm rang, she thought at first it was another dream till the ringing finally broke through her consciousness. There was no way she could go to work today. She called in sick then made coffee and listened to the sound of movement in Michael's room. Just a few more shopping days till Christmas, this was definitely not a good time to be calling in sick but she had a good staff. All of her seasonal employees were hired and trained. They'd be able to manage without her. What else was she to do?

"Any word from the hospital?" Michael asked as soon as he came out of his room. He was already dressed for the day, a very unusual phenomena considering it wasn't a school day, however not unexpected in light of yesterday's events.

"No, I was thinking about calling them." Diane called the hospital and was transferred to ICU when she requested Tom's room.

"I was calling to check on the status of Tom Wright," she said as a nurse answered.

"I'm sorry, I can only give that information out to family members."

"I'm his ex-wife. I was there with my son yesterday. We really want to know how he is doing."

"Okay. I see a note about you from last night on his chart. He's doing fine, slept through the night. We will probably be moving him to step-down later this morning as long as his body signs continue to remain stable. Fortunately the blow to his head didn't seem to have caused any damage to his brain. His liver is none too strong but functional. The cuts were all superficial. His heart seems to be stable, too."

"Thank you. Thank you very much. Will we be able to see him later?"

"Once he's moved, yes." Diane placed the phone down, filled with a strange mixture of apprehension and relief. She was relieved he was out of danger, but now she had to deal with seeing him and talking to him herself and Michael doing the same. What would she say after all these years? She prayed for guidance.

"What did they say?"

"He's stable and being moved to step-down today."

"Then will we get to see him?"

"Once he's moved to step-down."

"Let's go," Michael said anxiously.

"There's no sense in going right away," Diane began to explain, then seeing the look in Michael's eyes, she resigned herself to spending the morning in the hospital waiting room. At least they had coffee there. "All right," she grabbed her purse and coat. "I'm ready."

They drove in silence to the hospital. Diane resisted the urge to try to reach Jake. Much as she would like his calming presence right now, it probably wasn't the best idea. She and Michael needed to deal with this together.

They arrived at the hospital only to be told they would have to wait until he was moved, just as Diane had known would happen. At least Michael seemed to feel better sitting here than at home. Tom's wife joined them in the waiting area.

"I think maybe I should tell Tom you are here before you go in. Prepare him, you know," she said.

Diane agreed that was a good idea. Sadie went into step-down to help the nurses get Tom settled. Then she came out for Diane. Michael jumped up, preparing to go in. Sadie put her hand on his shoulder.

"He just wants to see Diane right now. He'll see you later, Michael." Diane was relieved to see that Michael had accepted this from her. She had been afraid he would insist on going in right away. Now that he was about to see his dad, Michael appeared less sure of himself.

"Sure. That's okay. I'll wait," he said and sat down.

Diane followed Sadie to the room. Sadie stopped at the door. "I'll be in the waiting room if you need me," she said. Diane appreciated Sadie's consideration of her. Tentatively she walked in. Tom's eyes were shut. She wondered if he was sleeping and whether she should wait.

"Tom," she called gently. He opened his eyes and smiled a weak smile.

"Diane, is that really you?"

"Yes it is." Diane came closer to his bed and sat down in the chair next to him.

"I couldn't believe Sadie when she told me. How did you find me?"

"Michael did. He's been looking for you for some time now."

"Michael, how is he?"

"He's fine. He's here. He really wants to see you, talk to you."

"Not like this, not looking like this. You look great, Diane."

"Thank you," Diane couldn't return the compliment. There were still traces of his boyish charms in his voice and his eyes but his face was lined and haggard and showed signs of the difficult life he must have led.

"How are you?" he asked.

"I'm fine. Really I am. And the kids are great. You'd be proud of them."

"You did okay by yourself, raising the kids alone?" he asked tentatively.

"Yes, I did okay. It wasn't easy but I managed. I missed you though." Now was not the time to bring up past hurts, the memory of all those difficult years wondering whether he would ever come back. "You never sent for us."

"I'm so sorry. So very sorry. I guess I wasn't cut out to be much of a father, or a husband either for that matter. I meant to send for you, I really did, but the time never seemed right and then so much time had passed, it … well, it was just too late." There was a long pause as Diane wondered what to say. Finally she broke the silence.

"Sadie seems like a nice person," Diane said tentatively.

"Yes, she's better than I deserve. She looks after me. I'm surprised she puts up with me."

"You still drinking?" Diane asked quietly.

"Just now and then. I fall off the wagon. Not like I used to be, though." Diane wanted to believe that.

"Michael wants to see you."

"I don't want him to see me like this, an old man, a beaten-down drunk."

"You owe it to him to at least talk to him. He is your son. It hasn't been easy, raising a son without a father."

"You never remarried?" Tom asked quietly.

"No, guess I never had the time. I was too busy with the kids."

"Was it that bad, life with me?"

Diane took his hand, "There were good times. I try to remember the good times. And at least I had the kids."

"Yes, the kids. What they must think of me? How they must hate me, abandoning them, abandoning you all these years. Do you hate me?"

"I did at one time, but I learned to forgive and move on. They can learn it, too. Michael can learn if you give him a chance. He really wants to see you. You owe it to him." Tom closed his eyes as if going to sleep. "Tom, you ran away from your responsibilities once. I won't let you do it again. Not now."

Tom opened his eyes. "It's okay. I guess I can see him. Send him in."

Diane went to the waiting room and brought Michael to see his dad. She stood off to one side with Sadie while Michael approached the bed.

"Michael?" Tom said tentatively.

"Yeah," Michael hesitated to call him Dad. After all this time it just didn't seem right. "Hi, how are you doing?"

"I've seen better days," Tom said with a small smile. "So how have you been? It's been so long since I last saw you. You're so big now, I'd hardly recognize you. Your mother speaks well of you."

"Yeah, well, I do okay. It hasn't been easy for her or me."

"I know, I know. I'm sorry, son."

Michael's eyes filled with tears. "What do you know about what it was like growing up without a dad? You always had grandpa."

"Yes, I did. I was very lucky. I don't think I ever really appreciated my dad and all he did for me."

"Yeah, well, that's over. He was kind of like a father to me. That helped."

"I'm glad to hear that."

"I tried to find you before, when I was a kid, but I couldn't."

"I didn't want to be found."

"But I wanted to find you. So now I've found you."

"That you have," Tom shifted uncomfortably.

"Maybe things can be different now, between us, you know."

"Maybe son, but don't count on it. Don't count on me. Can't you tell I'm not someone who can be counted on? It doesn't mean I don't care." Tom turned in the bed, avoiding Michael's stare.

"It's all right. I don't need a lot. I won't ask for much."

"Sure, son, sure," Tom was looking very tired. "Maybe we can talk again."

"Yeah, Dad," Michael finally used the word. "Yeah, I'd like that."

"We better go, Michael," Diane said. "He needs his sleep."

"Sure. I'll come back tomorrow. I'll see you then."

Sadie escorted them out of step-down. Diane gave her their phone number. "If there's any change, give me a call. If there's anything we can do to help, just let me know," she told her before leaving.

"You want something to eat, Michael?" Diane asked as they drove home.

"No, I'm fine. I've got to get to work soon anyway."

"You sure you want to work? You could call in sick. After all it has been a rough couple of days for both of us."

"No, Mom, it's all right. Do you think you could take me back to the hospital tonight, though?"

"Sure, Michael, whatever you want."

She dropped him off at work then returned home. Maybe I should go to work too, she thought. It would take my mind off of all of this.

There were messages from both Jake and John on her answering machine. As she prepared to return the calls, the phone rang again.

"Diane?"

At the sound of his voice, Diane felt all of the strength she had gathered to get her through the morning seep away.

"Hi, Jake," she said.

"Are you okay?"

"No, I'm not," she said truthfully, "but I will be. I just need a little time."

"Did Michael see Tom today?"

"Yes, we both did. It seemed to go okay. I'm not sure. You never could tell with Tom. Michael went to work."

"You want to talk?"

"Yes, I do," Diane was relieved to hear the suggestion. Now that he had offered it seemed like just what she most needed at this moment in time. "Can we meet for coffee?" They agreed to meet at a local coffee shop in half-an-hour. Diane was relieved to have an excuse to stay away from work. She decided to wait to call John later, when she felt more settled.

"How did you find him?" Diane asked as they talked over coffee.

"It wasn't easy, but it helps to have connections at the police station."

"Why wasn't the detective able to do that? That's what he was paid for, isn't it?"

"I guess he didn't have the right connections. Apparently Tom had been arrested on drunk and disorderly conduct charges at different times in the past. They ran a check on him and found out he was really Tom Price."

"What else did they know?"

"Not a lot, not really. No big offenses. Just small arrests here and there. It seems Sadie has done him some good. She helps him stay sober by getting him to go to AA meetings, but every now and then he falls off the wagon, gets drunk and gets into a fight. He has actually been able to hold down a job for the past year or so. So how's Michael doing with all of this?"

"I don't know. He's not saying much. I think he's confused."

"That's to be expected. He's a good kid. Been making me think about my own kids."

"Regrets?"

"Yes and no. I still don't regret leaving. I just wish I were part of their lives still."

"It's not too late."

"I don't know."

"Christmas is a good time for renewing acquaintances."

"I know. I've been thinking about that. Thinking about sending them a card or something, just a short line letting my kids know I'm thinking about them." Jake stirred his coffee aimlessly.

"Sounds like a good idea."

"I've also been thinking about you."

"Oh, in what way?" Diane stared down at her coffee, avoiding his eyes.

"Thinking about what I said the last time we met. Thinking maybe I was out of line. Thinking maybe, maybe we can be friends?" He reached across the table and covered her hand with his.

"Just friends?"

"Maybe more than friends."

"Christmas is a good time to renew old acquaintances. I'd like that," she said with a smile, still avoiding his eyes.

"So, maybe I'll call you?"

"And maybe I'll say yes when you do," Diane finally looked up and allowed her gaze to meet his. Their eyes held for but an instant. It was Jake who looked away first.

"I suppose I better go," he said reluctantly.

"And I better get back to the apartment. I told Michael I'd take him back to the hospital after he got off of work." After a moment of silence, Jake removed his hand from hers and said good-bye. Both were reluctant to have the moment end, but knew it had to.

When Diane returned to her apartment there was another message from John on her machine. She decided she better call him before she picked up Michael.

"I stopped by the store and they said you had called in sick."

"I had to take Michael to the hospital to see his dad this morning. We're going back again tonight."

"I had thought maybe we could meet for dinner."

"I'm sorry. I promised Michael."

"Then how about lunch tomorrow?"

"Sure, John, I can do that."

Michael didn't stay long that night. He seemed more at ease than that morning and seemed to feel better knowing he would have time to get to know his dad. Michael was already making plans for when his dad got out of the hospital.

"Mom, do you think you could invite Dad and Sadie over for Christmas dinner?"

"I guess that could be arranged as long as your dad feels up to it."

"Can I invite them tomorrow?"

"Sure, Michael, but I won't be able to take you tomorrow. I can't miss another day of work."

"That's okay. I can take the bus."

Michael seemed happier than he had been for years. Perhaps something good would come out of this after all, Diane thought. It was almost too good to hope for. She was in better spirits herself at work all morning. She had almost forgotten her lunch appointment with John till he came to pick her up.

"Is it lunch already?" she said with a smile as he walked in.

They dined at her favorite restaurant and lingered over coffee as they caught up on each other's lives. Diane was in no hurry to get back. "After all, what good is being management if you can't enjoy a long lunch now and then," she said with a smile.

"It's good to see you so relaxed," John said.

"I guess I'm just happy about Michael."

"It has nothing to do with me then," John stated.

"Well, I …" Diane muttered in surprise as the conversation took an unexpected turn. "What do you mean?"

"I mean, this isn't working, is it?"

"What isn't working?"

"Us, this relationship."

"Why would you say that?" Diane said slowly.

"You know if I thought your good mood today was because of seeing me, I'd say there was a chance, but we both know it's not true."

Diane's heart gasped. Did he know about Jake?

"I've been gone for three weeks, and yet it hardly seems like it has made any difference to you," John continued.

"I have missed you."

"But not that much. Isn't that true?"

"Well, I've been busy."

"Not that busy. It's almost as if you were relieved to have me gone."

"In some ways I have been. I haven't had to think about your proposal. I haven't wanted to think about it."

"And that's exactly what I thought. Have you given it any thought? Any real thought?"

"Some, I have thought about it some. I just haven't really felt ready to think about it. I'm still not ready to move. Not this school year."

"But it's more than that, isn't it?"

"Yes, I guess it is." She might as well admit it both to herself and to him, she thought.

"It's not working, is it?"

"No, I guess not. I'm not ready for marriage, not to you anyway. I'm sorry, John. I wish I were. I really do care about you."

"But not enough to marry me. That's okay, I'd rather have the truth," John said as she avoided his gaze. True to form, always the gentleman, he was doing what he could to make this easier on both of them. "I am a patient man, but I know when it's time to cut my losses."

"I'm sorry. I didn't mean for it to end like this, not at Christmas."

"That's okay. I've got family to spend Christmas with, then I return to L.A."

"So this is it? We can still be friends, can't we?"

"I guess so, from a distance, but still friends. Besides we still may have to work together." John paid the check and tip and stood up.

"Speaking of work, I guess it's time for me to get back," Diane said as she stood up. They drove in relative silence back to the store. Their only conversation consisted of clichés related to the weather, work and the holidays. She kissed him as she left his car. He didn't come into the store with her.

Diane was saddened at the end of this relationship, even though she knew it had been inevitable. Yet in some ways she was relieved. No more worrying about her feelings for Jake or feeling guilty about them. In many ways it was a relatively painless ending to the relationship. She was grateful for that.

Michael continued to be in a good mood as he visited his dad in the hospital.

"Do grandma and grandpa know you are here?" he asked his dad.

"No, and don't tell them," Tom insisted.

"But they would like to see you. Maybe they could come for Christmas," Michael added.

"Trust me, son, it's better this way," Tom said.

Michael finally agreed to not call them just yet. "Maybe when you are feeling stronger."

"Yeah, maybe then." That was as much as Tom would agree to.

Tom was scheduled to get out of the hospital on Christmas Eve. His injuries had proven to be less serious than had originally been thought and he was recovering much quicker than anticipated. He and Sadie had accepted the invitation for Christmas dinner. Adrian didn't know about the sudden turn of events, but she could be told easily enough when she got there on Christmas Eve. Diane had even invited Jake for Christmas. As long as they were having guests, what was one more? Besides Michael knew Jake and liked him. He had been instrumental in finding Michael's dad. And it would be a shame for Jake to spend Christmas alone. It seemed like a good idea.

Diane left a message for Jake at the Salvation Army inviting him over for Christmas dinner and was pleased when he left the message on her machine that he accepted her invitation. The apartment would be crowded, but after all, it was Christmas. Perhaps it would be a good Christmas after all.

Adrian was not only surprised to hear that Michael had found their dad; she was not too pleased about it.

"He shows up out of the blue after thirteen years, and not only that, you had to track him down. Now he's showing up for Christmas dinner with his new wife. Doesn't sound like much of a Christmas to me," she complained. She was not happy about being there in that apartment. She was not happy about anything right then.

Diane tried not to let it bother her. She focused on Michael's happiness.

"And who is this Jake guy you've also invited?"

"Just a friend," Diane explained.

"What happened to John? I thought he was more than a friend. Now this Jake character shows up."

"Things didn't work out with John. We both realized that. We're still friends. Jake is just a friend. I've invited him for Christmas dinner. What's wrong with inviting friends over for Christmas, especially those who don't have family available?"

"I don't know. I don't like the sound of it. I'm not happy about it."

"Yes, I know that. We all know that. Look, it's just for one day. In fact just a few hours for one day. Can't you please be pleasant for a just a few hours on Christmas?"

"All right. I'll try for your sake, Mom, but I don't like it."

Diane tried not to let Adrian's attitude bother her. Instead she focused on Michael and how happy he had been these last few days.

She had invited Jake to join them for the Christmas Eve service. She thought it would give Adrian a chance to meet him before seeing her dad again. It's not a good idea to have too many surprises at once, she thought.

Jake arrived at the church and slid into the pew next to her during the first carols of the night. Michael smiled and nodded his acknowledgement of Jake. Diane whispered an introduction to Adrian. Adrian gave him an icy glare at which Jake's eyebrows raised in question to Diane. She shrugged her shoulders and smiled crookedly as if to say, "I don't know what's going on with her." She squeezed Jake's hand to make up for her daughter's glare. Jake appeared to take it in stride.

As she sat next to her children and Jake and listened to the familiar carols and the so often heard story of the birth of a baby, she felt a glow of peace. Perhaps this would be a good Christmas after all, she repeated to herself.

After the service, Diane had a chance to more formally introduce Adrian to Jake. Adrian reluctantly shook his hand but refused to smile as she stated "Pleased to meet you" in a tone that indicated she meant no such thing. Still Jake warmly shook her hand and smiled despite the cold reception.

"Do you want to come over for a snack?" Diane asked Jake. "We've got Christmas cookies and eggnog."

Jake looked over at Adrian, then declined, saying, "No, thank you. I'm sure you three have a lot of catching up to do. I'll be over tomorrow, though." He squeezed Diane's hand and warmly shook Michael's and Adrian's hands as he wished them a Merry Christmas and took his leave of them.

"So what does he do for a living, this mystery man of yours?" Adrian asked as they drove home in the car. For a second Diane had to check and make sure it wasn't her mother speaking.

"It's no mystery. He's a janitor and he works with street people, helping out at the Salvation Army and the North-End Soup kitchen."

"Hmmm," Adrian muttered. Diane waited to hear a derogatory remark about his prospects but none was forthcoming. Perhaps because it was Christmas, Adrian managed to hold her tongue this once.

"That's how he was able to help me find Dad," Michael chimed in from the back seat of the car.

"No mean accomplishment that was," Adrian responded under her breath.

"Look, if you are going to be like this all day tomorrow, why don't you just leave. Maybe you don't care about seeing Dad tomorrow, but I do. Don't ruin it for me." So much for a peaceful Christmas, Diane thought.

"Look you two, please don't start fighting. It's Christmas. It's not like we have that much time together. Let's not ruin what time we do have with fighting."

"Well no one asked me whether I wanted Dad back in my life. I wish I had just stayed at school," Adrian said.

"Then why don't you return there," Michael retorted.

"Maybe I will, first thing next morning." There was an icy silence between the two of them. Diane turned on the radio to some Christmas music and began to hum along.

"I wonder what Santa will leave for kids who fight on Christmas Eve?"

"Come on, Mom, we're not babies anymore," Adrian said.

"Yeah, Mom," Michael echoed.

"That's funny. You could have fooled me."

"Oh, all right, Mom," Michael smiled. "I guess we can declare a truce for one night. Just no more comments about Dad. Agreed?" Michael reached his hand forward to the front of the car in a gesture of reconciliation.

"All right," Adrian said reluctantly, "Truce." She shook his outstretched hand.

Diane whispered a "Thank you, God" under her breath as she pulled into her parking space.

They exchanged gifts after they got home and reminisced about other Christmases as they snacked on ham sandwiches, finger food and Christmas cookies. Michael gave up his bedroom so that Adrian could have a little more space and privacy while he slept on the couch. Diane felt some apprehension as she went to bed, but overall she was at peace.

Christmas morning was quiet and uneventful. Both Michael and Adrian slept late. Diane got up early to put the turkey in the oven. She woke up Michael and sent him to her room to sleep while she worked in the kitchen. She softly played Christmas music as she worked, folding Michael's sheets and blanket and picking up the living room. Then she enjoyed a few moments of silence in front of the Christmas tree. A light snow had fallen during the night. Not enough to cause any problems driving but enough to coat the streets and sidewalk.

Diane went over in her head all that she needed to do yet today. The turkey was stuffed and in the oven. She was going to make sweet potatoes. She had a cherry pie and cookies for dessert and a vegetable tray and a cheese tray for appetizers. There wouldn't be enough room to fit all of them at her kitchen table so she planned on eating buffet style. Jake was going to come over as soon as he finished serving Christmas dinner at the soup kitchen. Diane had thought about volunteering to help out but thought better of it as she recognized all she still had to do. Also, this time with both of her children home together truly was precious. She didn't want to miss any of it.

Diane heard movement in the apartment as Michael got up and took a shower. She decided it was time to get busy making breakfast.

"Can I help with anything?" Michael asked as he walked out of the bathroom towel-drying his hair.

"You can watch the bacon while I take a shower," Diane told him as she pulled the turkey out in order to bake blueberry muffins. "Also, keep an eye on these muffins."

"Sure thing, Mom." Diane quickly showered and got dressed, then knocked on Adrian's door to let her know breakfast was almost ready.

The morning passed by quietly. Jake arrived at two and quickly set about making himself useful. He helped Michael set up a few extra chairs and set plates and silverware on the table for the buffet. Even Adrian helped some. Her plan was to eat at four. Tom and Sadie were supposed to come around three

When three came and went with no word from them Diane started to worry. As awkward as it was going to be having them here, it would be even more awkward if they didn't show up at all. She decided to put the appetizers out anyway so they could snack as they waited. Michael began to get agitated. What little good will Adrian had been able to gather for this meeting was rapidly dissipating. At three-thirty Jake helped Diane get the turkey out of the oven to let it set for a half-an-hour before carving. "Do you think we should call?" he whispered to her.

"That's probably a good idea," Diane agreed. "I'll make the phone call from my room." Just then the phone rang. Michael rushed to answer it, then thought better of it and decided to allow his mom to take the call.

"Hello?" she said as she put the receiver to her ear.

"Diane? This is Sadie. It looks like we aren't going to make it after all."

"Is something wrong?" Diane asked.

"No, no, nothing's wrong. It's just that Tom really isn't up to going out much just yet. Maybe we can do it another time."

"Sure, sure, I understand. Tell Tom we all said hi." Michael moved towards the phone indicating he wanted to talk. "Is Tom available? I think Michael would really like to talk to him."

There was a pause on the line before Sadie responded. "He's sleeping right now." Diane watched Michael's agitated movements.

"How about if we come over later? We could drop off some turkey. There's plenty here. I'd hate to see it go to waste."

"No, that's not a good idea," Sadie stated.

"How about tomorrow? Could we come by tomorrow?"

"Sure. I think that would be okay. I'll call you."

"Please do that."

"Oh, and Merry Christmas."

"Merry Christmas to you, too," Diane said as she slowly put down the receiver. "That was Sadie. They can't make it."

"I knew it. I knew he wouldn't show. He's just coming up with excuses. He doesn't want to spend Christmas with us any more than I wanted to spend it with him," Adrian snapped. "Well, I say good riddance. We're better off without him."

"Adrian, stop. He is your father. He's just gotten out of the hospital. It's understandable that he might not feel up to going out," Diane said.

"It's just a convenient excuse. He didn't want to be found. Just wait. He'll disappear again."

"That's not true," Michael shouted. "He's not going to disappear. Not now that I've finally found him. He probably figured you'd be like this and that's why he didn't want to come over. It's all your fault," Michael lashed out at Adrian.

"Michael! That's not fair. It's no one's fault. He's just not feeling too well yet. We can go visit him tomorrow," Diane intervened.

"He's probably been drinking. Too much Christmas cheer," Adrian commented dryly.

"But why couldn't I talk to him for just a minute?" Michael asked.

"Sadie said he was sleeping," Diane replied.

"Sleeping it off," Adrian muttered.

"Adrian, that's enough out of you. I'm not going to let this ruin
our Christmas dinner. You two stop it. Michael you can try calling
your dad later tonight. And now, since it's just going to be the four
of us, let's set the kitchen table and sit down together like a family.
Jake would you pull the table out?" Diane asked, trying to take
control of the situation.

Jake jumped to her assistance, pulled the table out and began to
arrange place settings. Diane cleaned the stuffing out of the turkey
and finished preparing the sweet potatoes. Jake set the turkey on the
table as Diane lit the candles and put on some more Christmas
music. Jake asked Michael if he cared to carve the turkey but when
he got no response, Diane nodded to him to do it.

"Jake would you say grace?" Diane asked quietly as they all sat
down.

"Lord, God," Jake began, "we ask you to bless this food and all
here gathered around this table. Bless also those we love who can't
be here with us." Jake paused as he remembered his own children.
"We thank you for this bounty and the many blessings you have
given us in our lives, and we remember those who are less fortunate
than us. Keep them safe in your care, Amen."

"Amen," Diane echoed. "Thank you, Jake."

It was a relatively quiet meal. Neither Adrian nor Michael were
talking much, although Adrian became more talkative as the meal
wore on, just as Michael became more sullen. Jake was asking her
about her classes and her job at college. He seemed to be drawing
her out. Now that Michael was looking so upset, she was starting to
regret the things she had said and was trying to make things up by
being more cordial. Diane allowed Jake and Adrian to carry most of
the conversation as she silently worried about Michael.

When dinner was over, Jake and Adrian helped her clean up
while Michael sulked. Finally he asked, "Do you think I could call
now?"

"Sure, Michael, go ahead." Diane knew what he had been
waiting for.

He went into her bedroom for privacy as he made the call.
Diane could tell by the disappointed sound of his voice and the way
he looked when he came out of the bedroom that he had not talked to
Tom.

"Sadie said he was still sleeping," Michael said before anyone could ask. "I'm going out for some fresh air," Michael said as he grabbed his coat and went to the door.

"Michael," Diane called to him.

"Don't worry, Mom, I won't be gone long. I'll be back," he assured her as he left.

Diane stood motionlessly for a few minutes.

"I'm sorry, Mom. I never should have said those things to Michael. I'm real sorry. I don't have to go back to school tonight if you want me to stay," Adrian said.

"But I thought you had to work tomorrow?"

"I can call in sick. It won't hurt any."

"No, I don't want you to do that. Michael and I can work things out."

"But Mom . . ."

"It's okay, Adrian. I can handle it. You do what you need to do. Go on, get your stuff together. I don't want to have to worry about you, too, driving home at night."

"Okay, would you tell Michael I'm sorry?"

"Sure, Adrian." Adrian went to Michael's room and finished packing her things as Diane fixed her a care package of cookies and leftovers from dinner.

"I put in extra for your room-mates," she said as she gave it to Adrian.

"Thanks, Mom, thanks and Merry Christmas."

"Merry Christmas, dear. Now drive safely."

Diane sighed as Adrian shut the door.

"Seems like just yesterday the two of them were just small children, so excited about Christmas. There were some rough Christmases, especially right after Tom left, but still they were so special. They grow up so fast," Diane commented and sat down on a kitchen chair.

Jake finished drying the dish he held and put it away.

"They're good kids. They'll be okay. Thanks to you."

"I was so afraid this might happen if Tom came back into their lives. It just brings back all the old hurt."

"But maybe now it has been brought to the surface, it can finally be healed," Jake said as he sat down.

"I don't know. Some things never heal." Diane paused and took Jake's hand. "I'm sorry you had to go through all of that, but I'm also glad you were here."

"I'm glad to be here." They looked into each other's eyes for a while in silence, both too tired to speak. The door opened and Michael returned. Diane let go of Jake's hand.

"Michael?" she said.

"I told you I wouldn't be gone long. Is Adrian gone?"

"Yes, I didn't want her driving home too late. She said to tell you she's sorry for what she said."

"That's okay," Michael dismissed the comment. "We can go over and see Dad tomorrow, right?"

"Sure we can. As soon as I get out of work, we can go over."

"Can't we go sooner?"

Diane paused and thought, "Sure, I'll take a long lunch hour."

"Thanks, Mom. I'm going to my room. Merry Christmas, Jake," Michael said as he shook his hand.

"I need to be leaving too," Jake stood up. Diane escorted him to the door.

"Thank you," she said as they held hands, then said good-bye.

"Good-night, Michael," Jake shouted across the room. "I'll call you tomorrow," he whispered to Diane as he gave her a good-bye hug.

Chapter 15

Diane wasn't sure what to think about the events of yesterday. Sure, it made sense that after just getting out of the hospital Tom wouldn't want to go anywhere or see anybody. Still she suspected there was something more going on. She wasn't sure what, but she had been suspicious. For all the years that had passed, he was still Tom. How much, if any, had he really changed? She wasn't sure. Much as she would like to give him the benefit of the doubt, she remained cautious about doing so. She just didn't want Michael hurt. That was her main concern.

It came as no surprise when Sadie told her Tom still didn't want any visitors. She could take it, but she wondered how Michael would react.

"We don't have to stay very long," Michael said when Diane called him from work with the news.

"I know, Michael, I told Sadie that."

"I'm going anyway, with or without you." Diane had been afraid that was what Michael would say.

"Michael, there's plenty of time. What's one more day?"

"I'm going. Are you driving me or do I have to find my own way?"

"I'll be right home. Don't go anywhere," Diane said.

He was waiting outside her apartment building as she pulled up. He climbed into the car without a word. It took Diane a while first to locate the apartment building Sadie had told her they lived in, then to find parking. Michael impatiently tapped his fingers on the door of the car. He almost bolted for the building as she parked the car, then seemed to think better of it and waited for her.

"You do the talking, Mom. Sadie will listen to you. Tell her it will just be a minute."

Diane rang the doorbell then waited as she heard movement in the apartment. The building was old, but not too run down. It wasn't the best part of town, but it also wasn't the worse.

Sadie opened the door and peered through the crack between the door and door frame, a chain lock still holding the door secure.

"Who is it?" Diane could hear Tom's voice calling from another room.

"It's Diane," Sadie called back then said to Diane. "I told you he doesn't want visitors."

"Couldn't we just see him for a few minutes? Michael has a Christmas gift for him." Michael stepped forward so Sadie could see him and his gift.

"Just a minute," Sadie said and closed the door. Diane could hear a muffled conversation going on.

"I don't want them to see me, not here, not like this," Tom moaned.

"How is this worse than the hospital?" Sadie asked.

"It isn't, I just, I can't deal with it, baby. You have to help me here."

"You can't avoid them forever."

"I know, but just not today. I can't deal with it today."

Sadie paused for a while, then finally agreed, "All right, but when will you see them?"

"Tomorrow, tell them tomorrow."

Sadie went back to the door and opened it a crack again. "He said he'll see you tomorrow. He just doesn't feel well enough today."

Michael seemed to accept that. "Would you give him this?" he showed Sadie the Christmas gift he had brought.

"Sure I will," Sadie said. She unlocked the door then came out into the hallway with them, shutting the door behind her. "Look, you seem like real nice folks. I don't know what Tom's problem is but come back tomorrow. I'll make sure you get to see him tomorrow," she assured Michael as she took the gift.

"Thank you," Michael and Diane both said to her. "We really appreciate it," Diane added as she grasped Sadie's hand with both of her hands.

"It's nothing," Sadie said as she hurried back inside. Diane could hear Tom calling her. "I've got to go."

They rode back in relative silence. "Sadie is real nice, isn't she?" Diane said to break the silence.

"Yeah," Michael agreed.

"Your dad's probably still a little tired."

"Yeah, sure."

"You want me to drop you off at work?" Diane asked before letting him off in front of the apartment building.

"No, I'll take the bus. See ya," Michael said as he climbed out of the car. She watched him go inside then decided she better get back to work. Christmas flowers from John had been delivered while she was gone. The note with them read, "Just because. Hope you had a nice Christmas, John." How sweet, she thought. She began to have second thoughts; maybe she had made a mistake. Maybe she shouldn't have let him go so easily. Where else would someone her age find someone so understanding? She pushed the thought out of her mind as she got back to work, checking on how all of the returns and exchanges of Christmas presents were going.

She came home to an empty apartment, except for the cat rubbing between her legs begging for food. Michael was at work. There was a message from Jake on the answering machine. Diane picked up Samantha and rubbed her under the chin while she listened to the message.

"Hi, Diane. I called to thank you for dinner yesterday. Hope everything is well with you. I'll try again tomorrow."

This time her heart didn't thump dramatically as she listened to his voice. Instead her mind returned to the image of the flowers on her desk and John. What was she doing, she asked herself. Am I only attracted to men once they are unavailable? It didn't make any sense to her. Funny how quickly feelings can change from one day to the next. Or am I just too upset right now to think clearly about anything?

She decided to pen a thank you note to John. "Thank you so much for the flowers. You are so thoughtful. I hope I can see you again next time you are in town, love, Diane." Should she tell him she had made a terrible mistake, or had she? She was so confused. Right now a comfortable, stable relationship with John felt like just what she needed, but that wasn't what she had thought a week ago. Had she just thrown away the best thing in her life for a whim?

She resisted the urge to write more, to tell John she had made a terrible mistake and wanted him back in her life. It was just panic, she told herself. Fear made a person do strange things. But fear was no way to live a life. Fear of being alone, fear of being vulnerable and unsafe, fear of the unknown – she couldn't live a life of fear. Was she reacting to fear or was it love? Was she afraid of the future, afraid of trusting again? Once burned, twice shy. She had trusted Tom so many years ago, but then, how much had she really known him back then? He broke her trust in so many ways. Dare she trust again? Could she trust again? Could she trust Jake, or John, or anyone? Better to stay in her protective cocoon than to take a chance on love.

She tried not to think about any of it. Men, what good are they anyway? They only cause you grief. She had enough grief dealing with Michael. She didn't want to think of any of it, but it was hard not to, sitting alone in her apartment with only a cat for company.

Jake called, "How are you? How's Michael? Is everyone okay?"

How did he know everything wasn't okay? He was the last person she wanted to talk to right then. Everything was so confusing. He just made her even more confused.

"It's okay."

"Did Michael get to see his dad today?"

"No, but he will tomorrow. He's okay with it."

"You don't sound okay."

"No, I'm okay," she lied, "I'm just tired. After Christmas let down, I guess. I just need some time to myself."

"Are you sure you don't want some company?"

"Yes, I'm sure," Diane told him. Now she was lying to Jake. What was she doing? She wanted some company, but who she really wanted to talk to was Marge. With Marge everything wasn't so confusing. She was her link to her past and a good friend. Marge would know what to say to help her feel better, make sense of everything. She tried calling Marge at home only to be told she was out for the night. "Her bridge club is having its Christmas get-together tonight. I'll tell her you called," Marge's husband assured her.

No luck, Diane thought. "Just you and me," Diane said to her cat as she picked her up and went to sit on the couch. The cat jumped out of her lap and walked away with her tail up. She would decide when and where she would deign to lie down. "So, even you don't want to have anything to do with me," Diane said with a slight smile. She sat and gazed at the Christmas tree without really seeing it.

Memories of past Christmases flooded her mind; Christmases when the kids were young; her first Christmas with Tom in their small makeshift apartment. They had been so young and in love. Still even then he was showing signs of alcoholism. She wanted to remember only the good times, not the bad, not his drinking, not the fights.

She remembered Christmases when the kids were babies, wondering when and if Tom would show up. He always showed up eventually and always with a convenient excuse. And then all of those Christmases when he wasn't around. She had learned to depend on herself and no-one else. She wasn't about to change that now. Not after all these years. No matter how lonely she was. She had made it on her own. She could continue to do so.

All those memories, some good, some not so good. It hurt to remember, to have them all come back. She had thought she had dealt with them, and yet here they were, unwelcome, unbidden, with feelings just as strong as if it were yesterday. But yes, it had been yesterday when Tom didn't show for Christmas. Just like all of those others yesterdays. And she was left, making excuses, dealing with her children's hurts.

"Damn him," she yelled at the tree. "Damn him and everyone who looks like him." Why did he have to come back to cause problems? She hadn't been looking for him. He hadn't been looking for her. It was Michael. Why did he have to bring this man back into both of their lives? Why? Why couldn't he have left things the way they were? It has brought nothing but heartache for both of them. Maybe it will work out. Maybe it will be okay. Maybe it will end up for the best. But something inside her, past experience with Tom, didn't believe it.

She was woken out of her thoughts by the sound of Michael coming home.

"Hi, Michael, how was work?"

"It was work."

"Are you hungry? Can I fix you something?"

"No, thanks, Mom. I ate something at work. I'm just going to listen to some music then go to bed."

"Sounds like a good plan," Diane said as he disappeared into his room, leaving her alone again, and yet not entirely so.

"What time are we going to Dad's tomorrow?" Michael's head appeared out of his room to ask.

"I guess around noon again. We can go on my lunch hour. I'll call you before I leave work."

"Okay," Michael said then popped back into his room.

She decided not to call Sadie before coming over this time. She didn't want to give Tom a chance to make up any more excuses. She and Michael knocked on the door a little after twelve. Once again Sadie opened the door with the chain lock still in place.

"Oh, hi, I thought you were going to call." Michael gave Diane an incriminating look. "Tom just stepped out. I told him you would probably be here soon. He said he was just going to walk to the corner to get a paper."

"How long ago was that?" Diane asked.

"About fifteen minutes ago. He should be back any time now."

"Can we come in and wait?"

Sadie paused to think, then said, "Sure," and let them in. The room was clean and neat. The furniture, while well-worn, was also well-kept. Sadie kept the place up as much as she could, Diane could tell. She knew it wasn't Tom who kept everything picked up. At least not her Tom.

"Would you care for something to drink?" Sadie asked as they sat down.

"No, thank you," they both replied. "This is a nice place," Diane added.

"Thank you. I try to keep it nice. Tom likes it that way." They sat in an awkward silence as Diane tried to think of something more to say. She noticed an afghan on the couch.

"Did you make that afghan?"

"No, it was from my grandma. It's very old. My mother gave it to me. Wherever I go, I keep it with me. It's part of what makes wherever I live a home."

Diane nodded her head in understanding to let Sadie know she knew where she was coming from. They sat in awkward silence for a while longer.

"I don't know what's keeping Tom," Sadie said then stood up. "I'm going to fix myself some tea. Are you sure you wouldn't like any?"

"Maybe that would be good," Diane said. At least it would give her something to do besides just sitting in this awkward silence, she thought.

"Are you sure he was just going for a paper?" Diane asked after twenty minutes had gone by.

"That's what he said. I don't know where he may have gone."

"I really have to get back to work," Diane said to Michael. He had sat in silence the whole time. He was unwilling to leave.

"I thought he knew we would be coming back around noon," Michael stated.

"He did. He knew that you were coming back today and that it would probably be around noon. I don't know what's keeping him," Sadie said. Michael reluctantly agreed to leave.

"I'll tell him you were here," Sadie said as they left. Michael maintained a surly silence all the way home. Diane didn't even bother to ask if he wanted a ride to work this time. She knew the answer already.

"How late do you work tonight?" she asked as she dropped him off.

"Six o'clock," he muttered.

"Maybe we can go over again then." When he didn't respond, Diane added, "You know, Michael, if you push too hard, your dad might run."

Michael didn't respond as he climbed out of the car.

Six o'clock came and went, no Michael. Then seven o'clock, still no Michael. It didn't take an hour to get home. Diane knew that. Perhaps he's talking with friends. Perhaps he's working over because someone didn't show up. That has happened before but each time Michael had called and let her know. No, she knew something was up. At seven-thirty she called over to the Stop and Go to see if Michael was still there.

"No, he left at six o'clock as soon as he finished his shift."

"Did he say anything about where he might be going?" Diane asked.

"No, but he did seem to be in a big hurry, like he had some place to go."

"Thank you," Diane said as she hung up the phone. What to do now, she asked herself. She had a pretty good idea where Michael had gone. He had gone to see his dad. Clearly he didn't want her along or he would have told her. Should she call over and find out if he was there, she wondered. She didn't want Michael to think she was checking up on him, but she was. When eight o'clock arrived and still no Michael, she decided to call.

"Hi, Sadie, this is Diane. Is Michael there?" she asked, trying to sound calm.

"He was here but he left an hour ago."

"Okay. Did he say anything or indicate where he might be going?"

"No, he didn't stay too long. Just talked to Tom for a short while. I don't know about what. Then he left."

"Thank you," Diane said as she slowly hung up. Maybe he had a hard time catching a bus home, she thought. He's probably on his way. She jumped as the phone rang.

"Oh, Jake, hi, I thought it might be Michael."

"Is something wrong?"

"No, it's just Michael didn't come home after work. He went over to see his dad and still hasn't gotten home yet."

"He's probably on his way. Do you want me to come over?"

"No, I'm okay. I'm sure he's just on his way. He'll be here any time now." Just then she heard the door open and Michael walked in. "He just got here. I have to go," she said as she prepared to hang up.

"Sure, I'll call later," Jake said in reply.

"Who was that?" Michael asked in a surly tone of voice. "You checking up on me?"

"No, it was just Jake. So how are you? Did you see your dad?"

"Yeah," Michael mumbled something then went to the kitchen. He took a swig of milk out of the cartoon then went to his room.

"Did you eat?" Diane called to him. "Do you want anything? How was your dad?" Michael ignored her questions and went to his room.

Diane wondered what was going on but decided to let it be. Michael didn't come out of his room although she heard him in the kitchen around midnight. He was still in his room when she went to work the next morning. She tried calling him at home around eleven but only got the answering machine. Either he was there and not answering the phone or he had gone out. He was working a lot of hours over Christmas break but she knew he wasn't scheduled to go in until two.

"Michael, it's Mom. Would you please pick up the phone if you are there?" She tried not to sound like she was pleading with him.

On her lunch break she decided to go see Tom and try to find out what was going on. Sadie didn't appear too surprised to see her.

Diane had not called ahead. She didn't want to give Tom a chance to sneak out.

Sadie let her in without a moment's hesitation. "Just a minute and I'll get Tom," she said. Sadie shut the door to the bedroom as she went in to get him. Diane could hear her arguing with Tom then she came back out. "He'll be with you in a minute," Sadie said.

Tom came out wearing a beat-up brown bathrobe over his pajamas. "I apologize for my appearance, but, you know, I'm still recovering," Tom said as he walked in.

"That didn't keep you from going out yesterday," Diane commented.

"Well, the doctor said some fresh air would do me good. Sorry I missed you yesterday."

"No, you're not. Look, Tom, what's going on here?" Diane didn't have time to waste.

"What do you mean?" he asked.

"I mean, I know Michael came by to see you yesterday. He wouldn't talk to me about it but was in a foul mood. What did you say? And why have you been avoiding both of us?"

Tom sat forward on the couch and hung his head between his shoulders as he talked. "I didn't say much of anything."

"You must have said something to upset him."

"Look, Diane, I know I wasn't much of a father. I guess I just wasn't cut out to be one. I can't just start being one now."

"But you are a father, his father. Would it be so hard to at least act a little like one now? It's not like Michael is five years old and needing you to teach him how to play baseball or anything. All he wants is the chance to get to know you."

Tom got up and walked around the back of the sofa. "I just can't handle this, Diane, can't you see that? I can't just pick up like the past thirteen years haven't happened."

"No one's asking you to," Diane said with compassion. "Is it too much just to talk to him?" She stood up and walked over to Tom.

"Yes, it is," he said with some anger. "I can't handle the recriminations, the why did you leave me, where were you all my life while I was growing up?"

"Nobody's saying that," Diane said softly.

"No one has to say it. It's there without a word being said. Look, you better go. I need my rest. Sadie will show you out." Tom started to walk to the bedroom. Diane grabbed his arm.

"That's what you did last night, isn't it? You showed him the door. This is our son, your son, Tom. You didn't have to raise him, I did, but you will not walk out on him again. You can walk out on me, but not your son," Diane said angrily.

Tom took her hand off of his arm. "Sadie, will you show Diane out?" he said as he walked to his bedroom.

"I think you better go," Sadie said quietly. "Give him some time," she whispered, "he'll come around."

"That's what I've been thinking for the past thirteen years," Diane retorted bitterly, "but he won't, he won't come around. Michael is just going to have to accept it," Diane said as she let herself out.

Diane called the store and let them know she wouldn't be back that afternoon. She didn't know where she was going to go. It was far too cold to wander around outside. She didn't know where Jake was, or even if she wanted to see him. After all, if he hadn't helped Michael find his dad none of this would have happened. Finally she decided to try church. She was pretty angry at God right then too, but at least it was a quiet space inside out of the cold.

She let herself in by the side door and pulled her coat around her as she sat down. It was chilly inside but better than being outside. The parish couldn't afford to heat the building during weekdays when it was not in use for church services.

She was too angry to cry, too angry to sit still, so she got up and walked around. Maybe a good long walk was what she needed after all to get out all of the pent-up frustration and anger, she thought. She was about to leave when she was stopped by a voice. This time it wasn't Jake, but she recognized it anyway. It was the church pastor.

"Can I help you?" he asked, "Diane, right?"

"Yes, I guess I haven't really taken the time to introduce myself properly."

"That's all right. I've noticed you. Would you care to sit down?"

"Yes, no," Diane fumbled for words. His eyes were kind and he had a warm strong feeling about him that reassured Diane, but she was reluctant to share her troubles. She wished it was Jake she was talking to, and yet she was relieved it wasn't. With Jake she wouldn't have to start at the beginning, but wasn't Jake part of the problem too, part of the whole mess?

"I don't know what to say. I'm sorry. I can't talk to you right now. I'm so angry and upset and I'm angry at God. I shouldn't be talking to you about this," Diane rattled on.

"You think God can't handle your anger? Let him hear it. There's nothing you can say that he hasn't already heard. God loves to listen to his children."

"He doesn't want to listen to me right now."

"Oh, yes he does. It's precisely at times like these that God most wants us to turn to him, anger and all. Don't hold anything back."

"I can't, I just can't," Diane fought the tears that seemed so close to the surface the last few days. "I'm just . . . My life is such a mess right now and I don't know who to turn to or what to do."

"Then turn to God," he replied warmly, taking her hand.

"I can't, I just can't right now. I'm sorry. I have to go." Diane took her hand out of his and rushed to the door.

Now she really had nowhere to go. Nowhere to be by herself, except her apartment, but she didn't want to go there. She felt sorry for how she had treated her minister but she just couldn't take his caring right then, couldn't handle it. She had no-one to turn to . . . but Jake. Maybe Jake could help. Maybe he could help her get her act together enough so she could talk to Michael.

She drove to the Salvation Army. She sat in her car for a few minutes before getting up her nerve to go in.

"He should be here in a half-an-hour or so. Do you want to wait?" the receptionist said.

"That's okay. I'll wait in my car."

"No need to do that, honey. Why not stay here where it's warm? You can go into the chapel if you want some privacy," she said with a kind smile. Diane had had enough of chapels for the day, and yet she found herself obediently following the kindly receptionist to the chapel.

"I'll tell Jake you're here as soon as he shows up," she told Diane as she opened the door.

Diane slowly walked in. Guess the die is cast, she thought. I can't leave now, not without being seen. She walked slowly about the chapel. This time she felt a little less restless and more able to sit. She chose a warm spot where the sun showed in through a window. She let the warmth of the sun warm and soothe her jagged nerves as tears slipped down her cheek. She couldn't remember how long she sat there before Jake came. It seemed like just a few minutes and yet an eternity. She wiped away the tears as Jake approached. He sat next to here and held her hand for a while without saying a word.

Finally he broke the silence. "Do you want to talk about it?" he asked gently.

She nodded her head, yes, keeping the tears she had allowed to slip out in the quiet of the chapel at bay. "Tom told Michael he didn't want to see him."

Jake handed Diane his handkerchief to wipe the tears. "Did he say that?"

"I doubt that he used those exact words, but the message was clear. Michael came home very upset last night so I went over to talk to Tom. That's pretty much what he told me. I don't know what to say to Michael. I'm so angry at Tom and so hurt for Michael. I don't know what to do."

Jake put his arm around her and held her. After a while he asked, "Does Michael know you went over there today?"

"No, he would be furious if he knew. But I had to find out what happened and I knew Michael wouldn't tell me."

"Some things a man's got to work out for himself. You know, Michael really is a man now. He's not a child. He can face hard realities and deal with them."

"So you think I was wrong to go over there?" Diane pulled away from him.

"No, no," he pulled her back close to him. "You had to do what you needed to do, but Michael has to do what he needs to do for himself right now. You can't do it for him."

"Oh, Jake, I had hoped and prayed that Tom had changed. I wanted so to believe that after all these years he had changed, that he would want to be a part of Michael's life. I guess I was wrong." Jake continued to hold her as she spoke. "And I thought, 'all things work for the good for those who love God,' right? I thought it had to work out, but now it isn't working out."

"This too can work out, Diane. You can get through this. Michael can get through this. Some good can come from this. You just have to believe and trust and continue to love God. With God's help, good can come out of the worst situation."

"But what do I do now? Should I tell Michael I know what happened between him and his dad?"

"Let Michael come to you if he wants to talk about it. You have to let him work this out. In the meantime you have to take care of yourself in all of this. We can't have you getting sick, can we?"

Diane smiled at this, "I'm all right. I'll be all right as long as Michael's all right."

"No, that's for Michael to take care of. You have to take care of yourself. Will you do that for me so I don't have to worry about you?"

"I can take care of myself, Jake. I've been doing it for so many years."

"Then you keep on doing it."

"I guess I ought to get home," Diane said as she sat forward.

"Only if you want to."

"No, I don't want to. I think I'd like to stay here for a while. If that's okay?"

"That's perfectly okay. Why don't you stay here while I do a little work, then we can get something to eat."

"No, I better not. I want to be home in case Michael calls. I want to be home when he gets home. I probably better go."

"If that's what you need to do to take care of yourself."

"Yes, I think this is what I need to do. Thank you for the offer though."

"I'll offer again," Jake said with a smile.

"And I'll accept," Diane smiled back. Jake walked her to her car. "I'll be in touch," he said as she closed the door.

"I know you will," she replied. Diane felt better for having talked to Jake but was unsure about what would await her at the apartment. Michael should be at work. That would give her some time to get her thoughts together.

There were no notes from Michael when she got home. Diane thought about what Jake had said about taking care of herself and decided to indulge herself in a bubble bath. The warmth of the water, the fragrance of the bubble bath and the feel of the bubbles on her skin helped ease away some of her tension so that she was almost relaxed when Michael got home. Once again he chose not to talk to her but retreated to his room. Diane wasn't entirely okay with this behavior, but she accepted it. She remembered what Jake had said about giving Michael a chance to work it out for himself.

Diane was surprised the next day at work by a phone call from Sadie. "Diane, I'm sorry to call you at work, but I didn't know what to do."

"What's wrong?" Diane asked.

"Michael came over here again today. He insisted on seeing Tom. It was like he just had to have it out with him. Tom didn't want to see him, but Michael was so insistent. I was afraid he would break the door down. So I told Tom he had to talk to him. They had angry words. Michael told him he walked out on him once but he would not let him do it again. He said he would keep coming over until Tom acknowledged him as a son and treated him like a son. Oh, Diane, he was so angry. Tom just couldn't deal with it. I'm afraid of what he might do."

"Is Michael gone?"

"Yes, he left a short while ago. Tom left too. I'm afraid he's going to go off the wagon again. I don't know what to do."

"I don't know either, but thank you for calling."

"Tom says you've got to get Michael to stay away."

"I can't do that, Sadie. You should realize that. This is between Tom and Michael. They have to work it out between the two of them."

"I don't know what Tom will do."

"Thank you for calling. Let me know if anything else happens." Diane slowly put down the receiver. What do I do now, she wondered? Do I talk to Michael or wait for him? What would Jake say? If only I knew what to do, she thought.

Chapter 16

"Jake, I feel so helpless," Diane was relieved to finally hear his voice. She had been so afraid when she called that she would hear the familiar refrain, "He's not here right now. Can I take a message?" Instead she had been put on hold for what seemed like an eternity.

"What's wrong?"

"Everything," she said.

"You're going to have to be more specific."

"I'm sorry. I'm just so upset and so relieved to hear your voice. I can hardly think."

"What happened?" At the sound of caring in his voice she almost burst into tears.

"It's Michael. He had a big fight with his father. Sadie called me. She said I've got to get Michael to stay away. Jake, I don't see how I can do that. Michael's too old for me to tell him what to do."

"That's right, Diane. This is something the two of them, Michael and his dad, have to work out for themselves."

"But what if Michael's dad isn't willing to work it out?"

"Then Michael will have to deal with that. There is nothing you can do but stay close by, let Michael know you are available, but don't push. Do you know where he is?"

"No. He didn't show up for work."

"Do you want me to look for him?"

"No, you're right. Michael needs to work this out himself. If I go out looking for him or send someone else out looking for him, he'll just have an excuse to be angry with me. Besides, he'll probably come home any time now."

"Do you want me to come over?"

"I don't know. I guess not. I guess I'm okay."

"Just because Michael needs to work this out for himself, doesn't mean you have to be alone."

"I don't feel alone, thanks to you. Thank you for the offer. Let me see how things turn out."

Diane hung up the phone and began her lonely vigil. Six o'clock. Seven o'clock. Eight o'clock. The hours dragged by. What was he doing? Had he gone back to his dad's? Was he just wandering the street? Was he at a friend's house? Diane didn't know any of his friends to call. She called back over at the Stop and Go to see if Michael had showed up there. No luck. Jake called back periodically to see how she was doing. At eight thirty the doorbell rang. Diane's heart jumped. Could it be the police? It couldn't be Michael. He had a key. He would have just let himself in. She opened the door a crack then opened it wide with relief when she saw Jake. He was holding a deck of cards.

"I know what you said, but I decided even if you could handle waiting alone, I couldn't. There was no sense in both of us sitting up alone worrying. Want to play cards?"

"Sure," Diane said with a smile.

The time passed much more quickly with Jake around, still with the tolling of each new hour her heart sank deeper into its worry. Nine o'clock. Ten o'clock. Finally at eleven she heard the door open.

"Michael," Diane called.

"Mom, I'm sorry you waited up for me."

"I called your work. They said you didn't come in for your shift."

"I came over to keep your mother company," Jake added.

"Yeah, well, I had a lot of thinking to do. I'm going to bed."

"Is that what you've been doing?" Diane asked. Jake put a calming hand on her lest she shift into interrogation mode. "I've been so worried."

"Yeah, well, I'm sorry, Mom. I really don't want to talk about it right now."

Jake's grip on her hand tightened as if to warn her not to pursue the matter right then. His eyes told her there would be enough time in the morning.

"Okay, maybe we can talk about it in the morning."

"Yeah, thanks Mom. I'm going to bed."

"Good night," Diane said.

"Good night," Jake chimed in. "I'm glad to see you home safely."

"Yeah, good night," Michael said as he walked to his room and shut the door.

Jake left shortly afterwards, after reassuring Diane that now was not the time to talk to Michael about it.

"Wait till you've both have had some time to think about this," he had told her.

Diane had thought about not going into work that morning. New Year's Eve. She was only scheduled to work till noon because of the holiday so she decided she could do that much. She could talk to Michael that afternoon before he went to work, or if not then, she had all of tomorrow to talk with him.

About ten o'clock she received another phone call from Sadie. Sadie spoke in a hushed voice. "I don't want Tom to know I called you. He didn't want me to call, but you seem like such a nice person, I felt like I had to."

"What's going on?" Diane asked in alarm.

"We're leaving. I told you I didn't know what Tom would do. Michael came over again last night. Tom can't handle it. We're leaving the city. Tom says he disappeared once before, he can do it again."

"Where are you moving to?"

"I can't tell you. If Tom found out he'd never forgive me. Maybe later, once we are settled, maybe I'll send you our address, but Tom, he wants nothing to do with it. Maybe he'll think better of it after some time."

"Where is Tom? Can I talk to him?"

"No. He doesn't know I'm calling you. He doesn't want to be reminded of his past. He's downstairs turning in our keys."

"But what about Michael?"

"I'm so sorry it didn't work out. You seem like such a nice person. I got to go. Tom will be back any minute now."

"But, wait. You can't just leave like this. What will I tell Michael?" Diane stopped as she heard dead air on the other end of the receiver. Slowly she put the receiver down. Her tears of yesterday gave way to anger. Anger at Tom, anger at Sadie, anger at Michael, anger at God.

"You say you care for us," she shouted inside. "You promised everything would work out. You promised. You're no better at keeping your promises than Tom is, or was."

Diane arranged to get out of work early. Maybe she could make it to Tom and Sadie's apartment before they left. Maybe she could stop him. She impatiently answered those business items that couldn't be put off and left without clearing her desk. I can always come back this afternoon, she reassured herself. But another half an hour and it may be too late. It may already be too late. Please God, don't let it be too late, she prayed. Please, please, God. For Michael's sake, let me talk some sense into Tom. Please God. She bargained with God all the way across town. She promised Him anything and everything, if only He would do this one thing for her, for Michael.

Her heart sank as she pulled into a parking place by Tom's apartment. Something told her she was too late. She knew it in her heart, but wouldn't believe it, could not accept it. She walked up the two flights of stairs to Tom's apartment, her feet feeling like lead. She rang the doorbell and knocked but no one answered. The sound of her knocking echoed throughout the apartment. She walked downstairs to talk to the building superintendent.

"The couple in apartment 314?" she began.

"They're gone. Left this morning. In quite a hurry. They didn't even want to take their furniture. Odd pair."

"Please, did they leave any forwarding address?"

"No. In fact they made sure everything was squared away with me before they left so I wouldn't be going after them. They forfeited their security deposit and the rent for next month, not to mention their furniture. He was in quite a hurry to leave. They're not in trouble, are they? You're not a cop?"

"No, no, no trouble. But is there any chance I could look around the apartment? Maybe I'll find a clue to where they went."

The man paused suspiciously, then looked Diane in the eyes and said, "Sure. I guess no harm will come from it. Come on."

Diane followed him back upstairs. He unlocked the door and let her in. Despite the haste with which they had left, the apartment didn't look ransacked. Sadie had kept a clean apartment and had left a clean apartment. There were very few personal items left amidst the furniture that she could see, still she needed time to look more thoroughly. The afghan was gone from its space, letting Diane know the residents were not coming back.

"Look, I've got to get back downstairs," the super stated. "Just pull the door shut when you leave," he paused. "You won't take anything, will you?" he added sheepishly. "I've got to ask, you know."

"No, I won't, at least not without asking you first," Diane reassured him.

"Okay," he said as he left her alone in the apartment. Diane proceeded to the bedroom, the apartment door left ajar. She wasn't sure what she was looking for, or what she might find. Maybe an address book, or a scribbled note with a phone number. Any clue to where they may have gone.

She was so busy about her task that she didn't hear the sound of another person in the apartment.

"Dad, Sadie?" She was startled at the familiar voice. Michael, she thought. Oh, no, what am I going to tell him?

"Dad, are you here?" Diane decided there was no sense in avoiding the inevitable. Much as she wanted to hide in a closet, she decided to tell Michael what had happened. Better now, better that she tell him than letting him find out through strangers. If only there had been time to call Jake. If only Jake were here. He would know what to do, what to say. She had to do it on her own.

"Dad, I came by to apologize for how I acted yesterday. Are you here?" Michael called out.

"No, Michael, he's not here." Diane came out of the bedroom and approached Michael.

"Mom, what are you doing here?"

"I'm sorry, Michael. Your dad's gone. Sadie called me this morning and said they were leaving. I wanted to get here in time to stop them, but I didn't. I tried. Your dad just couldn't handle it so he left."

"No, that's not true. You chased him away, didn't you? Why else would you be here right now? You never wanted me to find him in the first place. You told him to leave, didn't you?"

"No, Michael, that's not true. You can ask the building superintendent. They had left before I got here."

"I don't believe you. Sure we had an argument yesterday, but he wouldn't have left, he wouldn't have left me without saying goodbye, without saying something."

"But he did, Michael. He can't handle being a parent any more now than he could thirteen years ago."

"You're lying. I don't believe you. It's all your fault. It was your fault he left in the first place and your fault he left today. You drove him to it."

"No, Michael, please, you've got to believe me." Diane couldn't believe this turn of events. "Please, Michael."

"I don't believe you, I can't believe you," he said as he stormed out of the apartment. Diane was so confused. She had known it would be hard for Michael to accept his dad's rejection, but she hadn't expected this, hadn't expected to be rejected in return. After all those years raising him and Adrian on her own, was this what it had come to?

Diane sat in shock on the couch, her mind spinning, unable to make any sense of the situation. He was just hurt, just lashing out and she was the easy target, she told herself. Still the words burned in her ears. It will be okay, she told herself over and over again. It will be okay. Michael will come around.

That was where the building superintendent found her an hour later.

"Are you still here?" he asked, then added when he saw the look on her face, "Are you okay?"

"No, I'm not," Diane admitted.

"Is there anything I can get for you? Anyone I can call?"

"No, there's no one, no one can help me," she said in despair, then coming to her senses she realized how she must sound. "I'm sorry. It seems I'm always apologizing to someone. Now I'm apologizing to a complete stranger," she said partly to herself, partly to the super. She shook her head and stood up. "I guess I better go. Thank you for letting me look around."

"Are you sure you're okay? Do you need a taxi?"

"No, I've got my car. I'll be okay."

The man followed her out the apartment, wondering whether it was safe to let her drive in her dazed condition.

"You sure you don't want me to call someone?" he asked again.

"No, no, thank you for your help. There is one thing you can do for me." She reached into her purse for her business card. "If you hear anything from either Tom or Sadie, would you please call and let me know?"

"Sure, lady. No problem." He held the door for her as she left the building. "Oh, and Happy New Year," he called as she walked away.

It felt somehow comforting and reassuring to be back in her car. This was hers. This was familiar. She sat for a few minutes, trying to decide what to do next before starting the car. It was no use trying to find Michael, not in his state. He'd come home eventually, wouldn't he? She tried to reassure herself of this. He couldn't stay mad at her forever, could he? She thought about calling Jake, but he probably wouldn't be at the Salvation Army till after three. She could go to his apartment, but instead she decided to drive home. It would feel good to be in familiar surroundings. Besides she wanted to be there when Michael returned. At least now he knew his dad was gone. What he would do with that information was in his hands.

She was comforted by the presence of her cat as she walked in. Samantha rubbed up against her legs. Diane picked her up briefly as the independent creature wriggled out of her arms. "Must want food," Diane thought. There were a couple of messages for her from work. A couple of minor problems she hadn't had time to deal with this morning. She called, took care of everything that could be handled over the phone then told them she would not be back for the rest of the day. They could survive without her, she told herself as she hung up. She was strangely calm as she fixed herself a cup of tea and sat in the window seat. She let her answering machine take her phone calls as she listened for the one voice she longed to hear, that of her son. She knew it would be a long vigil.

She was surprised to hear John's voice come over the phone. "Hi Diane, got your note. Just wanted to wish you a Happy New Year." The sound of his voice evoked no emotion in her. Jake called three times before Diane decided to take the call.

"Diane, where are you? I called the store. They said you were home. If you are, would you please answer?"

Jake was about to hang up when he heard her voice respond, "Hi, Jake."

"Where have you been? I've been worried."

"I've been here. I just haven't been answering my phone calls. I didn't want to tie up the line in case Michael called."

"Diane, what's going on? Are you okay?"

"I'm okay. I have to be here for Michael."

"Where's Michael? You don't sound okay."

"I don't know where he is," tears started to stream down Diane's face as she talked and the numbness wore off. This was why she had not wanted to talk. "I can't talk right now," she told him. The tears that had been so close to the surface, that she had been fighting over the roller coaster of the past week, would no longer be denied.

"I'll be right over. Don't go anywhere or do anything," Jake said before hanging up. "Promise me you won't go anywhere."

"I promise," Diane stated docilely, tears still streaming down her cheeks. It felt good to finally let them flow rather than fighting them. "I'll stay here."

True to his word, Jake was over in twenty minutes. Diane found it hard to find the strength to walk over to the door and let him in.

He hugged her as soon as she opened the door, then led her to the couch and let her cry for a while before asking her any questions.

"Can you tell me about it now?" he asked gently.

Diane wiped her eyes and pulled herself up. "I've got to stop crying. Michael would hate it if he saw me like this. I can't be crying when he gets home."

"So what happened, where is Michael?" Slowly Diane told Jake about the events of the day.

"When did this happen?"

"I don't know, around noon, I guess."

"Why didn't you contact me?"

"I figured you wouldn't be around till three and then when I got home, I just couldn't think to do anything. I'm sorry."

"You don't owe me an apology. I'm the one who should apologize to you. You needed me and I wasn't there for you."

"No, it's all right. I knew how to find you if I wanted to."

"Still, I can't expect you to be running all over trying to track me down. Maybe it's time I got a phone of my own."

Diane said quietly, "So I can call?"

"So I don't miss important phone calls from important people in my life. You are important to me."

Diane wasn't able to comprehend the full importance of what Jake was saying in her present state of mind. All she could think of was Michael and how miserable she felt. Still it was comforting to have Jake there.

"Do you think I was wrong, going to Tom's apartment like I did?" she asked.

"Michael would have had to find out sometime anyway."

"But it must have looked so suspicious to him. No wonder he blamed me."

"Michael needed to strike out. You just happened to be the person who was available. He'll come around."

"I wish I could believe that."

"Hey, look, it's New Year's Eve. People all over the United States are going to parties tonight to celebrate the New Year. It looks like it's going to be another long night for both of us. We might as well make the best of it. Care to play a little strip poker?" Jake pulled out his deck of cards.

"Now wouldn't that be a nice welcome for Michael when he showed up."

"It might get his mind off of the scene earlier today," Jake teased. "Do you have any food around here? Playing cards makes me hungry." Jake got Diane busy in the kitchen as he put some holiday music on. They munched on sandwiches and snack food while playing cards. Jake tried to keep the conversation light and away from Michael as the hours continued to creep by.

"Look, Diane, it's New Year's Eve. Chances are Michael's at some party along with ninety percent of the rest of the population. He won't get home until at least after midnight," Jake reassured her.

After eleven Diane insisted she had had as much card playing as she could stand for the whole year. They turned on the TV to see what was happening in Times Square.

"It was just two years ago that I was there in Times Square, celebrating the New Year with all those people and yet all alone. Doesn't seem possible," Jake said.

"And I was home alone, watching the ball drop and wondering what my son was up to. At least now I'm not alone."

"Me too. It's funny how you can be so alone in a crowd." They sat on the couch for a while watching the TV.

"You know, the city is supposed to be shooting off fireworks at midnight. We might be able to see it from the rooftop. You want to try?" Jake asked.

Diane paused, wondering about leaving the apartment.

"What are the chances that Michael will show up at midnight?" Jake asked.

"Not very good," Diane admitted.

"We might as well enjoy ourselves." Diane agreed. They got on their winter coats, took the elevator to the top floor then walked the rest of the way to the rooftop. A few others had the same idea. They huddled close together on one side of the building. Jake led Diane to a more private spot where they could wait together in peace.

It was a crisp and clear winter night. The lights of the city couldn't completely drown out the star-filled sky, but certainly provided competition. Jake wrapped his arms around her and held her close for warmth as she shivered in the cool air. The thought of Michael, somewhere in the cold, invaded her mind despite her efforts to not think about him. She began to shiver some more and shake as she cried. Finally she blurted out.

"Oh, Jake, I'm just a failure. I'm a miserable failure. I've failed at everything that was truly important to me – my marriage and now my son. He's completely rejected me."

Jake paused before responding. "Maybe, Diane, maybe you are a failure. But if so, look at me. I'm a failure too. I didn't just lose my job, my home, my family. I walked away from them. All of them. Like a fool I threw it all away. And for what? For what? To find myself? To walk the street with the homeless? To share my life with those who are homeless? Certainly I was a fool. I had everything and I threw it all away. But did I really? Did I really have anything at all? A job that was empty, meaningless. A marriage that was dead. That was what I left.

"I feel worst about my children. I lost them in the process, but I found myself. I found out I was more than the paycheck I brought home or the house I provided. I was more than that, so much more. I was a child of God, loved by God, not for what I do, but just because of who I am. I lost everything, but I found myself. Would I do it again if I had it to do over? I don't know. Perhaps I would have done it differently. I would have found a way to maintain my relationship with my children. That is my only regret. But I don't regret what I've done with my life or who I've become. I've become me," Jake said. He waited a moment, staring out over the expanse of the city, before beginning again.

"Perhaps I am a failure. Perhaps I've lost it all, but if so, I'm in good company. I'm not a miserable failure, but a magnificent failure just like that man who walked this earth two thousand years ago, who died on a cross for us. A reject, a failure, but a magnificent failure and the light of his failure shines even today so many years later. I would rather be a failure standing in his light than have all the money in the world." Jake paused again and turned to look at Diane.

"I may be a failure but at least I know who I am and whose I am. I am a child of God, loved by God and that's enough. That makes all the difference. Do you see that, Diane? Can you see it? Can you believe it?"

As he spoke it seemed that all of the lights of the city around them went out and all she could see was the color of the fireworks bursting in the sky. Then brighter than all the fireworks an image of a cross filled the sky. It was a glorious sight. It rested there in time, ablaze with color and light and for just a moment, time stood still around her and she knew what Jake was saying not with her ears, but with her whole being. She knew the truth of it. That she was loved, incredibly loved. That Jesus had died not just for a bunch of strangers so many years ago, but for her. He had died for her, Diane Price. And that was enough.

She was no more of a failure than he had been because she was loved, loved so much that this man had been willing to die for her in a very personal way. He had died for her for this moment that she might know what it is to be loved as a child of God. Then the moment was over. Around her she could still hear the popping of fireworks but inside all she saw was that glorious vision of the cross. She knew that she was loved and she knew that her son would be okay. She didn't know how, but she knew he would be okay. This God who loved her also loved her son, more than even she did. He would be okay. She knew it.

She collapsed in her exhaustion and cried while Jake held her, not speaking a word. No words were necessary, just a strong shoulder to lean on. That was all she needed.

"Did you see it?" she finally asked.

"See what?"

"The cross ablaze in the sky? Did you see it?"

"Just rest," Jake said and held her tighter.

"It's going to be all right, Jake. It's going to be all right. I know it. God told me so."

"Just rest, you need your rest," Jake said. "Let's go back to your apartment so you can get some sleep." He pulled her close and led her docilely off of the roof, back down the elevator and down the hall to her apartment, his arm holding her to his side and supporting her.

"You go to sleep," he told her as he sent her to her room. "I'll stay in case Michael calls."

"It's going to be okay, I know it," Diane said and kissed him gently on the cheek before collapsing into a deep sleep.

Chapter 17

Jake spent the night on Diane's couch. He didn't think it was a good idea to leave her alone in her current emotional condition. Diane slept long and hard. He didn't hear a noise out of her till ten o'clock the next morning. As for himself, he slept restlessly through the night, listening for Michael to come home or Diane to wake up. In his wakeful moments he found himself wondering about his own kids, wondering what would happen if he tried to call them. They had been much older than Michael when he had left; still, how much of a father had he been to them when he had been living with them? He had spent all of his time either at work or business functions. How much time had he had with his children?

Michael so desperately wanted a relationship with his dad, but that was because he had never known him. His kids had known him, in a sense. They had known him to be so involved in work that he never had much time for them. They had known him and now had every reason to disown him. It was different. The two situations were different. Or were they? The thought kept nagging at him. Enough for now, he told himself. For now it's enough to focus on the present and the problems of the day. He had enough on his hands just helping with Michael. He could leave his own children till tomorrow.

He got up at eight and fixed a pot of coffee. He was already on his second pot when Diane finally got up. She appeared groggy and yet still at peace. Jake wondered about what she had said last night. She appeared to be slightly out of her mind, perhaps out of worry. She hadn't made much sense. All that talk about seeing things in the fireworks. He was glad she had slept through the night.

"Did Michael come home?" were her first words.

"You want some coffee?" Jake asked as he handed her a mug.

"Thank you. What about Michael? He didn't come home, did he?"

"No, he didn't. You feeling okay?" he asked.

"Yes, I'm fine. I'm fine. He's all right. I know he's all right. What do we do now?"

"I'm not sure. It's too soon to report him as a missing person. I can spread the word on the street to look for him. That may help.

I've still got favors owed me, but I'm afraid it won't be easy to find one teenage boy in a city this size."

"So when do we go?"

"*We* don't go anywhere. You need to stay home in case Michael comes back. I'll check in with you each hour. Probably the best thing to do is to just continue to wait and pray."

"Okay. You look terrible. Did you sleep at all last night?"

"Some, not a lot. How about you?"

"I slept soundly. You didn't see it, did you?"

Jake had been hesitant to bring up the events of last night. With all of the stress Diane had been under it was no surprise that she might be seeing things. He avoided her eyes.

"You don't believe me. You think I imagined it."

"You are under a great deal of stress."

"I wasn't out of my mind. I've never been so in my mind. I've never felt such complete . . . peace. It was real, more real than anything I've experienced before. More real than you, standing here before me," Diane took his hand as she said this.

"What exactly did you see?" Jake asked.

"It was a cross, a cross of fireworks blazing across the sky, brighter than any fireworks I've ever imagined. And in that second I knew everything would be okay. You don't believe me, do you? You think I imagined it." Diane began to have doubts herself.

"No, I believe you think you saw something. Diane, there are so many things in this life, in this world, that I don't understand, can't understand. Maybe this is just another one of them. There is more to this life than anyone can begin to imagine. There is a reality beyond this reality. Maybe you did have a glimpse of that."

"I don't care what you think. I know what I saw and I know it will be all right. No, I do care what you think, but that won't cause me to doubt myself or what I experienced."

"I wouldn't want it to. So, are you okay alone?"

"I told you I was."

"Then I guess I'll see what I can do about finding Michael. You sure you're all right here alone?" Jake repeated.

"I'm fine. Just find my son for me. Bring him home safely to me."

"I'll do what I can."

Jake had no idea where to start looking. It was a big city. But he figured he had to at least try. He had to do something for Diane's sake. He stopped by the Stop and Go where Michael worked and asked if anyone had seen him since yesterday. He asked about any employees he may be with.

"Maybe Nathan would know," a teenager working behind the counter with a portly middle-aged woman responded. "They seemed to be friends. Sometimes they worked the same shift. Sometimes he'd hang around and talk to Michael after his shift. Maybe he'd know something."

"Can I get his phone number?" Jake asked.

"Sorry," the woman, obviously the supervisor, answered. "I can't give that out, but he's scheduled to work second shift today. You can come back then."

"When is Michael next scheduled?" Jake asked.

"Not until tomorrow, but, I don't know. He missed one of his shifts this week. If he misses again, he may lose his job."

"If I find him, I'll let him know."

It wasn't much but at least it was something.

Jake called Diane to see how she was doing and see if she had heard anything.

"Nothing, not a thing," she replied to his question.

"You don't sound too good," he stated.

"I'm fine, just worried."

"It looks like there's not much more I can do here. I'm going to stop by the soup kitchen and Army – then I'll come back to your apartment for a while."

"If you think that's best," Diane replied. He said, yes, then hung up. Despite her peace of last night and this morning, worry was setting in again. She knew everything would be all right eventually, she just wished she knew when and how. It seemed as the day wore on all the life she had gained last night kept draining out of her till nothing was left. She found herself doubting what she had experienced.

Maybe I hadn't seen it, she thought to herself. Maybe it was just my imagination working overtime. But if it was, her imagination wouldn't have brought her such a sense of peace. No, whatever she saw, even if she had imagined it, the peace was real. The sense of

God's love, that was real. That was all that mattered. Diane reassured herself of this as she waited for Jake.

"You look terrible," Jake said as he walked in.

"You don't look any better. Have you eaten anything?"

"No, I'm not really hungry."

"Neither am I but we both should eat."

"I suppose so," Jake agreed. They went into the kitchen and fixed sandwiches. They ate in silence, both too worn out to speak. Despite her long sleep last night Diane was worn out from the strain of wondering and worrying.

"Why hasn't he at least called?" Diane finally asked.

"I don't know."

"It's not like him to not call, let me know he's okay."

"We just have to trust that he's okay and will call when he's good and ready to."

"I guess. At least when he ran away last summer, I knew he was in his hometown. Now he could be anywhere."

"Do you think he could have gone 'home' again?"

"I've thought about that, but I don't know. I don't think so. I think he'd be more likely to try to track down his dad again."

"No luck there either, unless he went back to their apartment again."

"But why?"

"Same reason you did. To try to find a clue about where his dad may have gone."

"Maybe. It's worth a try. Let's go."

"Wait, you stay here in case Michael calls."

"I can't stay cooped up in this apartment any longer. I have to get out."

Jake paused as he looked at the determined look on her face. "All right. We go together, but not for too long just in case Michael calls."

"No, we won't be long," Diane agreed.

They stopped by Michael's work place on the way to Tom and Sadie's apartment.

"No, I haven't seen him or heard from him, but I'll let you know if I do," Nathan said. Jake gave him Diane's number then they left.

No one was at Tom's apartment. They had both known it was a long shot. A neighbor responded to their knocks.

"They're gone," he said, "moved out yesterday."

"I know," Diane responded. "I was looking for my son. Have you seen him around?"

The man looked more closely at Diane. "Yup, I recognize you and the boy with you. That was your son?"

"Yes, have you seen him?"

"I've seen him around off and on all week."

"Was he here today?"

"No, but I think I saw him here yesterday. He was looking for the building superintendent. I told him he was gone for the day and wouldn't be back until tomorrow."

"If he comes back, my son that is, would you call me?" Diane gave him her number.

"Sure thing, ma'am."

"Thank you," Jake said as they left.

"Well, at least we know he was here and may come back if he didn't get what he was looking for," Jake said as they drove away. They drove home in silence and walked in silence to Diane's apartment.

"I'll go out and check again," Jake said as Diane opened the door. "I think it's better if you stay here, though, just in case."

"I know," Diane agreed, "but it's so still and lonely here." Diane looked around the apartment, first checking the light on the answering machine for any messages. "I don't remember leaving the kitchen light on," she commented. "Could it be . . . Michael?" Diane called, afraid to even hope.

Her heart thumped with relief as the familiar figure came out of his bedroom door.

"Hi, Mom," he said sheepishly. "Where have you been?"

"Looking for you. Where have you been?" Diane responded.

"Just around, thinking and all." Michael paused then continued. "I'm sorry about what I said yesterday, Mom, real sorry."

"That's okay, Michael, I know you were upset."

"No, it isn't okay. You've always been there for me, all these years. I never should have said those things to you. It wasn't your fault Dad left, not now, not any more than it was your fault when he left thirteen years ago. If it was anyone's fault, it was mine."

"Oh, Michael," Diane walked over to him and touched his arm. "It's not your fault."

"No, I should have backed off. I should have just let him be, given him some space."

"It probably wouldn't have made a difference, Michael."

"I just wanted so much to get to know him. I guess I got what I wanted, but it didn't turn out how I had expected. I know now, he just wasn't able to be the dad I wanted."

"Where did you stay last night?" Diane asked.

"The church. I didn't know where to go. The door was unlocked so I let myself in. Later I hid in the pews as the minister locked the building. He found me there this morning. He wanted me to call you but I talked him out of it. I promised him I'd go home. It took me awhile to build up my courage to go home, but I had promised." Diane hugged him.

"I'm so glad you kept that promise."

"I am too. I have to call him and tell him I'm here. He had me promise that as well."

"Then you go do that," Diane said, "You can use the phone in my room if you want."

Diane held onto Jake in relief while Michael made his phone call. "I can't believe he's actually here," she said. "Thank you so much for all of your help." Jake continued to hold her until Michael came back out of Diane's bedroom.

"I bet you're starving," Diane said as she pulled away from Jake.

"It has been a long time since breakfast. Rev. Adams treated me to breakfast before sending me home."

"I'll fix us something. Jake, you can stay, can't you?"

"I wouldn't miss this celebration for anything."

Diane thawed some hamburger and made some quick sloppy Joes with Michael and Jake's assistance.

"You know, Rev. Adams is quite some guy," Michael said.

"That so?" Jake replied.

"Yeah, he is. He said he has some maintenance and janitor work I could do around the church. Of course, he also tried to hook me up with the youth group, but I don't know about that."

"Might not hurt to try," Diane began. Jake gave her a look of caution lest she frighten him off by appearing too enthusiastic about the possibility. "Only if you want to, Michael," she added.

"Well, it might be a way to make a few new friends."

"Oh, by the way, Michael, if you want to keep your present job . . ." Jake began.

"I know. I missed my shift. I wonder if I still even have a job. I better call as soon as we are done eating."

"Good idea," Diane and Jake said in unison. They toasted the New Year with champagne Diane had bought for New Year's Eve. She even let Michael have a glass. "After all, it is a celebration," she said.

After dinner Michael called Nathan at work and found out what time he was scheduled to come in.

Jake excused himself, worn-out and yet relieved and happy after the turn of events.

"I don't know what the reverend said to Michael but it seems to have done some good," Jake commented quietly as he and Diane slipped outside her door to say good-bye.

"Thank you, Jake, so much for your help, for being there for me, for everything." Diane put her hands on his and gazed into his eyes. Slowly she reached up as he bent forward and their lips met in a warm kiss. Reluctantly they pulled apart, eyes still locked in a gaze.

"Maybe it's going to be a good year, after all," Diane said with a smile. "Thank you," she said once again then slowly went back inside her apartment.

Chapter 18

It was good to get back to work and some semblance of normalcy, whatever that may be. She had to make up for her absences over the past few weeks, but life was fairly smooth, at least as smooth as it could be with a teenager around. Diane never asked Michael any more about the events of that night or what he and Rev. Adams had talked about. She just knew that whatever happened, Michael seemed more at ease with himself and others. It was as if he had come to some acceptance of himself that day, and an acceptance of his dad.

Sadie finally wrote with their new address after several months. Diane shared the letter with Michael after writing and assuring Sadie that Michael wouldn't come looking for them. Michael did send his dad a birthday card and a Father's day card. It wasn't the relationship Michael had hoped for but at least it was contact.

Diane saw John again the next time he was in town on a business trip. They had a very pleasant lunch together but both realized that their decision to simply be friends had been a good one.

As for Jake, he got that phone as he had promised he would. Diane started to help out at the soup kitchen twice a week as she was able. Jake got a response from his Christmas letter to his daughter. Tentatively they began to rebuild their relationship – first via letters, then via email. He even attended her graduation. Diane had offered to come with him but he decided that at this point it was better that he go alone. It had been good seeing his daughter.

He had walked over to his ex-wife, Laura, her new husband Paul, and his sons standing outside after the graduation. The boys awkwardly accepted his outstretched hand.

"Good to see you, Dad," the oldest had said.

"Good to see both of you. How's college?"

"Oh, you know, college is college," he responded. "Hey, there's someone I got to see."

"Me too, but it was good seeing you, Dad," the younger added.

"Go on," Jake told them as they slipped off to join their friends.

"You look good, Jake," Paul said as he offered his hand. "How is life in the Midwest?"

"Slower than New York."

"Well, it must agree with you."

Jake leaned over and kissed Laura on the check. "You did a good job," he said, "raising them I mean."

Laura bit her tongue. The words, "no thanks to you," were swallowed. She didn't want anything to ruin her daughter's day. "Thank you," she said instead.

"Daddy," Elizabeth hugged him. "I'm glad you came."

"I'm glad too, sweetheart."

"Pictures, we've got to get pictures," Laura said, "Now where did those boys go?" She pulled out her camera for some quick pictures before Elizabeth said, "I've got to go. I have to get ready for our senior party. Will you be around for a while?" she asked Jake.

"A while, just till tomorrow afternoon."

"I'll see you then," she said as she hurried off. They met for lunch the next day, Elizabeth tired from lack of sleep. Still he thought the trip had been worth the effort.

Jake also attended Michael's graduation with Diane and Adrian. Diane had felt it was only right. Jake had been instrumental, if not in getting Michael to this point, at least in getting her there, through the difficulties of the past year. Michael didn't graduate with honors, but at least he graduated.

He was now working part time at the church and had become involved in the youth group. He was even dating a girl he had met through the church. He was still working at the Stop and Go as well and preparing to attend the local community college for two years before transferring to a four-year college. He was undecided about a career, but he knew he didn't want to spend the rest of his life working at the Stop and Go or any other place like it. Rev. Adams had become a friend. He seemed to think Michael would be good in ministry and encouraged him in that direction. Diane had her doubts but kept them to herself.

She and Jake and Michael had become regular church goers, warmly greeting Rev. Adams after each service. At first it had been a little awkward in light of Diane's encounter with him in the church after Christmas, but he never said a word about that and after all he had done for Michael, Diane couldn't stay away despite any embarrassment she may have felt. He warmly shook her hand that first Sunday back and told her how happy he was to see her.

Diane invited him and his wife over for dinner at times. Their children were grown and living on their own. It was nice to know that, yes, they do eventually move out. Not that Diane was in a hurry; still, perhaps there was life after children, a whole new life for her. She was anxious to know what it might entail. Adrian had finally brought her most recent boyfriend home to meet her. Diane wondered if marriage might be in the works but knew better than to push it. But grandchildren would be a nice addition to that new life she was awaiting.

Michael even received a card from his dad and Sadie for his graduation, although Diane suspected it was Sadie's doing. Diane was content with her job at the store. She had turned down a promotion in order to settle into a more permanent position at her present location. No longer in the manager-in-training track, she was now the assistant manager on a more permanent basis. She had taken herself out of the advancement track. She liked where she was, the responsibilities she currently had and her life in this city. She wasn't interested in moving.

With the warm summer weather, she and Jake were able to find time to enjoy the zoo, the park, and other outdoor attractions of the city, and each other. Diane found herself getting to know more and more of the street people Jake worked with. She extended a hand of welcome to them. There were still thorny times in their relationship as both adjusted to the idea of giving up some of the freedom and independence they had fostered over the years in order to be more interdependent. Still God seemed to bring them closer with each disagreement.

It was Fourth of July. Michael had a date that night. Adrian, the perennial student, was living where her college was year around now. Diane and Jake sat on her roof awaiting the fireworks display, toasting each other with sparkling wine. As they stood together, side by side, their arms around each other, gazing off in the distance, Jake finally asked her.

"So how about it?'

"How about what?"

"How about we get married?"

"I thought you'd never ask," Diane replied with a smile as she turned to face him and kiss him as the fireworks blazed about them and never ended.

Q & A on Magnificent Failure

Q – What led you to write *Magnificent Failure*?
A – My divorce. We tried to do everything "right" if that's possible, different from the characters in this book. We worked to do what was best for our children, co-parenting. It was one of those learning experiences, one I don't want to repeat. I learned a lot about myself and about marriage through my divorce. I had sought out counseling; still, I couldn't shake the feeling of being a failure in this very important aspect of life. So I decided to write about it. Through writing this novel, I was able to deal with my own feelings of failure and finally put them behind me.

Q – How did you come up with the title?
A – There is a book I had read many years ago called *Magnificent Obsession*. It was turned into a movie with Rock Hudson. The movie focused on the romance between the two stars, not the message of the book, which was about literally applying the passage from Matthew's gospel about keeping your good deeds secret. "And your Father who sees in secret will repay you." (6:4) The hero went around doing good deeds, making those he helped swear to secrecy. He then used those good deeds as "leverage" for other good deeds. Whenever someone would try to pay him back he would say he had already used it up and could not accept any recompense. It was truly a magnificent obsession to do good. When exploring failure, it occurred to me that Jesus' death on the cross was a magnificent failure, hence the name.

Q – You describe scenes at soup kitchens and homeless people on the streets in your book. How did you research this?
A – I lived it. In my twenties I had worked with street people at an overnight shelter and soup kitchen. Many of the characters and scenes for this came from those experiences.

Q – The turning point in your book is what some would term a mystical experience. Could you say more about such experiences?

A – I have found that mystical experiences are far more common than we are led to believe. We don't talk about them because it is considered unacceptable. Also, there is a sense that they are private and not to be shared. We talk freely about all aspects of our sexual life, yet are uncomfortable talking about God. Many people have had experiences of the transcendent, whether just a sense of a presence, a spoken word, or being transported to another reality by a beautiful sunrise or scene in nature. Our God is truly present in our everyday lives!

Note to the reader:

Did you enjoy reading this book? If so, please leave a review on Amazon. Your comments would be appreciated and mean so much to me in terms of helping others notice my book. You, the reader, have the power to make or break a book in this day of emarketing and social media.

Thank you so much for reading *Magnificent Failure*. May God bless you in all your new beginnings!

Patricia Robertson

Other novels by Patricia M. Robertson

Dreamweavers – Dream again, wherever you are in your life. An exploration of how our dreams change over the course of our lifetime. Join Kate, a single mom, her teenage daughter, Terri, and others as they seek out new dreams for their life.

Buying Time – Visit the peace movement during the Cold War era of Ronald Regan, SDI (Strategic Defense Initiative) and MAD (Mutually Assured Destruction). Join a rabble-rousing Catholic priest and Methodist minister, a kindergarten teacher, and a Quaker homemaker, as they beat swords into plowshares, or in this case, hammer on a B-52 bomber. Arrested and jailed, they bought the world time through doing time

Land of Deep Waters - Honduras, land of deep waters, a country torn apart by civil unrest, violence and poverty: Is it possible to go back? Thirty years after being banned from Honduras as a young nun, Joan, now married with two grown sons, finds herself haunted by memories of her four years there. She is determined to return, but how, and if so what will she find?

Dancing on a High Wire – What do you do when life knocks you off balance? Sara, a senior at Michigan State University, is looking forward to graduation and starting her life with her fiancé when he breaks off the engagement. Joy, a ballet instructor, is happily married and expecting her third child when she is diagnosed with breast cancer. Esther is planning on continuing at her current place of employment until retirement when she finds herself unemployed with few job skills. Each needs to find a "new normal" and regain their balance on this high wire we find life.

Coming in 2015 – *Still Dancing* – sequel to *Dancing on a High Wire*.

Robertson also is author of four non-fiction books and writes two blogs each week. For more information about her books go to www.patriciamrobertson.com.